GUARDIAN

VOLUME 4

THE GREAT FORGET FANTASY SERIES

TERRY IRONWOOD

All rights reserved. No part of this publication may be reproduced, stored or transmitted in any form or by any means, electronic, mechanical, photocopying, recording, scanning, or otherwise without written permission from the publisher. It is illegal to copy this book, post it to a website, or distribute it by any other means without permission.

Copyright © 2024 by Terry Ironwood

This novel is entirely a work of fiction. The names, characters and incidents portrayed in it are the work of the author's imagination. Any resemblance to actual persons, living or dead, events or localities is entirely coincidental.

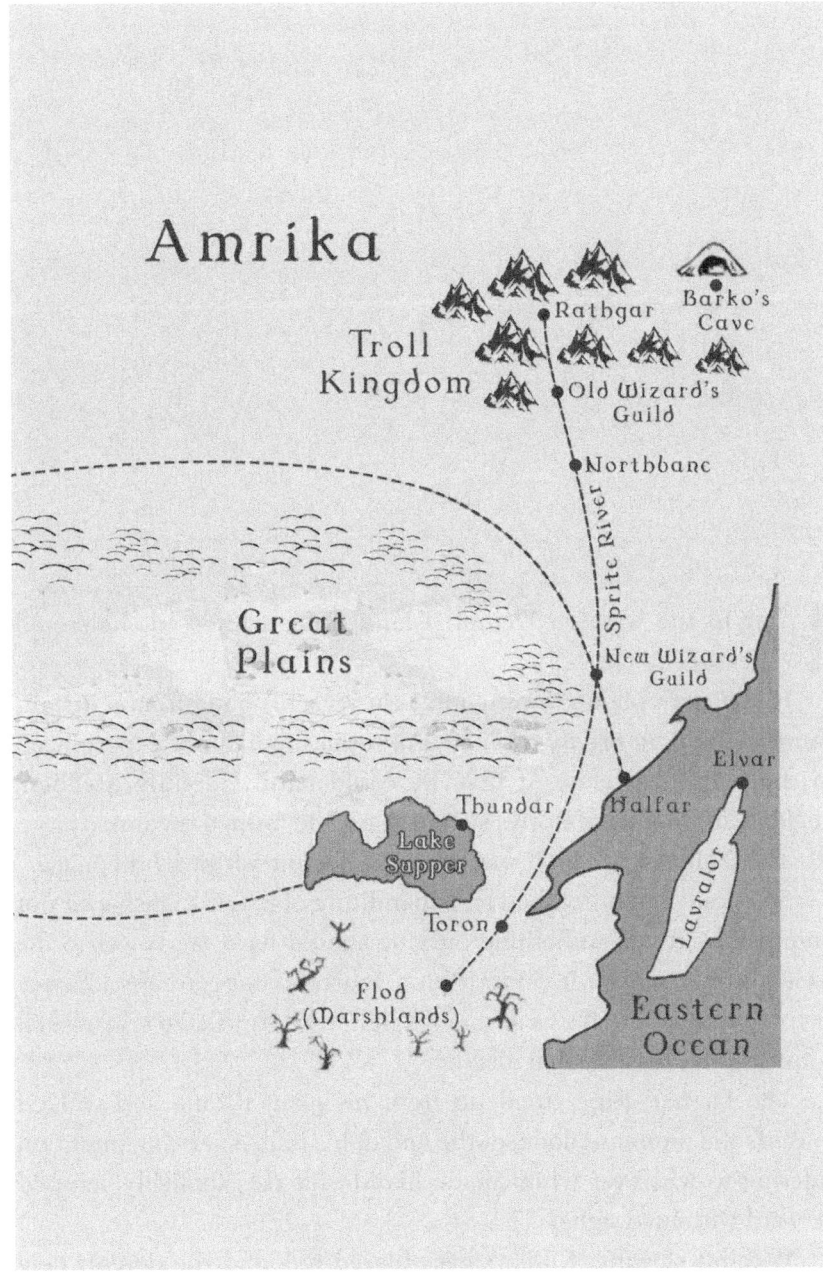

1

Far to the west on Demon Island, Killian lifted his helmeted head.

He felt a ripple of Power course through his body from a distant source. A feeling briefly overcame him that he had not experienced in thousands of years. At first, he could hardly identify it. Then, ancient childhood memories surfaced, and he formed the link.

The feeling was fear. It was brief and fleeting yet gave him pause.

Someone had unleashed an expenditure of magic that should not be possible. It was something only he should have the Power to do. Based on his senses, it came from a source about a week's journey east. No human or elf was strong enough in all Amrika to create such a disturbance to carry that distance.

The Demon King stood up from his giant throne and walked towards the immense doors at the end of his hall. A servant, intent on catering to whatever whim made his Master rise, foolishly stepped forward without a signal.

Without slowing, Killian's eyes blazed red, and the demon flew sideways with horrific force, slamming into the stone wall of the throne room to disappear in a cloud of black mist. The other servants lay on their stomachs, mewling with joy that they were in his presence, grovelling at his leisure. The Inner Circle bowed low, daring not to raise their eyes unless called. Typically, dawn signalled rest to prepare for the coming night, but he had been deep in thought on his rock throne, head bowed. The others waited on his eminence without moving.

He strode forward and nodded almost imperceptibly towards two large, heavily muscled demons, which immediately pulled open the massive hall doors to reveal an immense stone verandah overlooking the white, pulsating barrier. He had built his fortress on the easternmost point of the island on purpose, facing the white wall, nursing his revenge. The sun was cresting the horizon but not high enough to shine over his prison wall. The island was still shrouded in night, but the barrier, illuminated by the rising sun, shone with a white radiance.

The Demon King stood with black cape billowing, facing the object of his hate. Unable to control his anger, he lifted both gloved hands, eyes blazing with fury, and unleashed two pillars of red fire at the base of the barrier.

Every day, he worked tirelessly, in conjunction with the Inner Circle and his Dark Elves, to weaken the barrier, but someone daring to unleash magic that he had not authorized infuriated him. The red fire struck the base, and the whole barrier seemed to buckle under the attack, but it stabilized and absorbed the onslaught, for now.

The demons behind him in the fortress wailed in agony at their Master's rage. A few of the weaker ones ran screaming off the steep sides of the verandah, inconsolable with grief, falling hundreds of feet to their deaths. With his anger temporarily satiated, the Unnamed One lowered his arms.

He sensed the barrier weakening fast. It would not be long now. He had already waited three thousand years. Killian could wait a little longer.

The Lord of the Dark Elves calmed himself enough to assess the situation. There was only one being that might be able to unleash such magic. He was the Red-Eyed King under the city of Toron. Yet even as the thought entered his mind, Killian knew it was not so. The so-called king guarded great knowledge and would never leave the Ancient City. He would be dealt with in due time. A ripple of pleasure washed through him at the thought of burning the old king to dust before his eyes.

No, it must be the boy with red eyes. Could he be that powerful already? The child had allied himself with the young wizard who had stolen the orb. Xandrostika was his name. He was now likely an old man. The Demon King clenched a black, gloved hand into a fist. That wizard would suffer like no other, as would the boy who had managed to destroy General Morgo. He had to pause for a moment, trying to subdue his rage. He briefly thought of killing everyone in the vicinity but managed to control himself.

Morgo had been his most loyal and knowledgeable advisor. He had shown him how to harness the Power of the rare baby demons born with white eyes. Morgo alone could separate the Power from the life form so he could drink it. It was a complex ritual, but Killian had drunk it countless times over the millennia until his Power was so vast that he felt like the Creator. Yet even so, it was still finite.

None had been born with red eyes after him, only the human boy. He knew he had made a mistake underestimating the child. Even Morgo had paid with his life. Elohan and Marta were dead too. That almost made him angrier than anything else. He would have given much to personally torture Elohan to death for allowing his black dragon Fang to die. Being deprived of that joy made him furious. He had taken his wrath out on hundreds of lesser demons, but it was not enough. He would find this boy and make him pay.

That turn of events did give him pause. It caused him to delay a subsequent attack on Vanalon. He would now wait until ten thousand demons were able to cross then surround the city and annihilate every living thing. The reinforcements from the human city of Calgar were laughable. However, there was the possibility that the boy and the wizard were still defending Vanalon.

Then again, this new release of magic further east suggested otherwise. An improbable thought struck him. What if the magic he felt originated from his home in Cave Mountain?

Zoran had been recently sent there to feed the Dim and set it loose to kill the boy. Perhaps this red-eyed child and the orb-stealing wizard had unleashed all their magic upon the creature before being touched.

A pang of disappointment struck him at the thought. He would prefer to torture and kill them himself, but he had ordered the Dim to hunt the boy down. Now, he regretted his decision. However, the thought of the creature unleashed on the pathetic race of humanity imbued him with unbridled joy.

Killian resisted the urge to stride forth himself and lay waste to Vanalon. No, he would wait until the barrier fell then walk over the dead human skulls in his demon army's wake. He longed to stand before the smashed gates of Toron with a hundred thousand demons. They could feed at will while he would go deep underground and seize the knowledge that was his birthright. The Red-Eyed King would grovel at his feet and beg for mercy. He might even grant it. Yet the boy and the wizard, if still alive, would suffer. He trembled with ecstasy at the thought. First, he needed to know what caused the disturbance.

He raised a gloved hand. "Murk," he called without turning. His voice cut the air like a knife. The demons lying prostrate shrieked with joy that they had the privilege of hearing their Master speak. Murk scurried over to him and fell to his knees, eyes downward, grovelling at his leisure. "Rise," the Demon King intoned. His voice, deep and strong, exuded power. Murk stood up and looked at him, trying to hide his fear. This Dark Elf had a special talent among the Inner Circle.

"Master, may I grovel at your leisure?" Murk responded in the perfunctory way, bowing low.

"Find me the source of the disturbance a week's ride east."

"Disturbance?" Murk asked. The Demon King backhanded him across the face, cracking his jaw in two and sending the Dark Elf sliding senseless across the verandah's edge. Over the millennia, Killian's Power had grown to the point that it permeated his entire body so that even a physical strike was amplified.

Murk was lucky to be alive. Before falling to his death, the Demon King reached out with his Power and levitated the Dark Elf back to hover in front of him, unconscious. He healed him with his magic, realizing absently that Murk's skull was cracked, and he would have been dead in moments if Killian had delayed any longer. It would have been a shame to waste his unique attributes. However, Morgo taught him not to tolerate insubordination, so his reaction was appropriate.

Murk opened his eyes, fully healed, and bowed low as his king set him down. "My apologies, Master. I spoke recklessly."

"You must have permission if asking a question. I will not have this conversation with you again."

"Of course, Master."

"Good. Now, what is your question?" The Demon King was exercising patience, but even he had limits.

"Master, I humbly asked what you meant by a disturbance?"

The Unnamed One tried to remain calm. He thought of sending the elf to the dungeons to be tortured for a century but decided to give him one more chance. Besides, Murk indeed held a unique talent. "I have detected a strong magical anomaly a week's ride east, a disturbance, possibly near my home in Cave Mountain. I want you to investigate and report back to me."

Murk bowed low again, almost touching his head to the ground. "As you wish, Master, may I grovel at your leisure."

The Demon King paused. "Take the trackers with you. If you encounter the boy or wizard's trail, assuming they are alive, find out where they are headed."

The prophecy suddenly struck Killian like a lightning bolt. "Knowledge would be given when only one red eye is left." He cursed and involuntarily drew in more Power, causing his eyes to blaze a brighter red. Murk shrank back in fear, thinking he would be incinerated.

Killian ignored him. He had ordered Zoran to release the Dim on the boy, but now he desperately wanted to capture the child alive. Yet, the boy's death would guarantee that only the Red-Eyed King stood in his way to the knowledge of the Great Forget. Once the Ancient King was eliminated, Killian alone would know all the secrets. He could give the order right now to have the child assassinated. After all, Murk was his master assassin.

No, he decided, the Lord of the Dark Elves would have his vengeance. He reprimanded himself for even following such a weak train of thought. Ordering Zoran to unleash the Dim on the boy had been a moment of weakness. No one could stand against him, not even the Creator himself. "Capture the boy and kill his companions, especially those dear to him. Leave Arkan's pathetic spawn, the Orb Stealer, to me. If you kill the old wizard, you will suffer in his place. You are my only shapeshifter. They will not see it coming. Use the trackers to find them, then do what you do best, Master Assassin. Send one Tracker back to report your progress when you know where they are. If you fail, not even your soul will escape me. Leave now. I will open a passage for you."

"Yes, Master, may we grovel at your leisure," Murk said, fawning obsequiously.

The Demon King turned and walked back into his fortress, black cape billowing. The demons chortled in ecstasy at his return. He sat back on his great throne and looked out the open doors at the pulsating barrier. Killian slowly smiled, knowing the Age of Humankind was coming to an end. His smile turned into a deep laugh that reverberated off the stone walls. His Dark Elves and demons erupted with shrieks of joy, revelling in their Master's pleasure.

The sound reached the multitude of demons surrounding the fortress until the whole island exploded with a cacophony of noise.

The Age of Demons was at hand.

2

The companions spent the remainder of the morning climbing down the base of Cave Mountain. They were all exhausted but exhilarated. The Dim was buried under an immeasurable amount of stone. The feeling of being relentlessly chased was finally gone. They reflected on how draining it was to be in a constant state of fear and confinement. The weapons master was the only one unfazed. He had taught Chip that life was a set of tasks or challenges to be completed to promote growth. His mantra was that life happened "for us," not "to us." Taking that mindset freed a person from blame and suffering. Garth gave the boy a rare nod of approval when he came down the mountain after destroying half of it.

The others rushed up to slap him on the back, asking a flurry of questions until Xander finally told them to give the boy time to unwind. Chip looked at his companions with a tired but relieved expression and thanked them for the reprieve. They all agreed to continue walking until they were well off the mountain. The princess grabbed Chip's hand, beaming happily as she walked beside him.

The party traversed a long swath of rocky ridges that zigzagged down the east side of Cave Mountain. At times, they had to walk single file, picking their way down rocky precipices, before the ground started to even out and patches of rough scrub grass appeared.

Looking ahead, Chip felt awe at the vast emptiness of the Great Plains. They looked like an endless, brown wasteland extending to the eastern horizon. Xander said they would camp in the foothills that evening and reach the Great Plains by midmorning the next day. From there, it was a day's walk to Banfar, where they would pick up much-needed supplies.

The autumn air flowed crisp but began to warm as the sun rose. Chip wanted to ask the wizard questions, so Xander agreed to speak when they broke for lunch. The boy did not complain about exhaustion or lack of sleep, still digesting the enormity of the previous day's events. After his harrowing experiences in Fang Forest and Cave Mountain, he was happy to be alive and whole.

The sun reached its apex as they reached a small river at the mountain's base. The companions stopped to eat what meagre rations they had squirrelled away. Thankfully, the weapons master produced a hunk of cheese in a small side pouch while the wizard found a chunk of hard bread in the voluminous interior of his gray robes. They gratefully drank the cool river water flowing from the peaks. The stream would undoubtedly wind down to the mighty Rocky River, which flowed east to Calgar. The travellers found a flat grassy area with several large rocks in an almost perfect circle, providing an ideal spot to rest and eat.

They each sat on a stone, with the wizard sitting cross-legged in contentment on the green grass. The sun shone straight down, warming their tired faces. Chip listened to a soothing birdsong from a nearby copse of trees carried by the warm breeze. The haunting notes stood out against the backdrop of the gentle sound of the meandering river.

Chase broke the silence first, looking at Chip, unable to contain himself any longer. "How did you do it? That fireball took out half the mountain. I didn't think you had that much Power. What do you think happened to the Dim? Is it dead?"

"One question at a time," Xander admonished with a smile.

Chip laughed. "I had some help." He patted the pouch, holding the egg.

Xander's face turned serious. "Let me see." Chip unhooked the pouch and undid the drawstrings. Reaching in, he produced a perfectly oval, shiny white egg. Something about the purity of the colour was mesmerizing. He passed it to the wizard. The boy felt a flash of amusement come into his mind from the egg.

Xander handled it gently, turning it over to see all sides, a look of amazement on his face. "If you think the diamond throne was the most valuable thing in the world, you would be mistaken." He held the egg up into the light. "This is."

"What is it?" Chase asked in wonder as he leaned forward, almost falling off his stone seat.

"It is a dragon's egg," the wizard answered softly. Chip nodded to himself. It was as he suspected.

Chase's mouth fell open. "But you said they were all dead?"

Xander looked at him. "So we thought, my boy, so we thought." He rested the egg on the grass and stared at it. "The dragons died out during the Elf Wars, after the Breaking. They were formidable, majestic creatures, almost impervious to injury. Some were equal in strength to the mightiest wizards, but the elves turned them on each other. Over time, they fell one by one in great battles until none remained, or so we thought. When Chip destroyed the black dragon in front of the gates of Vanalon, I assumed it was surely the last one. Even the Dark Elves seemed to think so. Yet the Unnamed One is cunning and saved two eggs for himself, hiding them in the mountain." He paused, murmuring to himself. "It cannot be."

Chase leaned in. "What's that? Did you say something?"

The wizard looked up then shrugged. "I do not believe this is a normal egg."

"Why not?" Chip asked.

Xander turned to look at him and sighed. "Dragons are some of the most mysterious beings ever created. They hold great Power and are highly intelligent. They cannot speak as humans do, and only the elves can communicate with them through images." Chip was staring at the egg with a puzzled expression. With a start, he looked up to see the wizard watching him keenly. "No human has ever communicated with a dragon, much less rode one," Xander stated without moving his eyes.

"I can."

The wizard looked down to smooth out his robes, trying not to make a face. "Can what?" he asked in an even voice, looking up.

"I can communicate with this dragon," Chip said. Xander coughed to clear his throat. "It also linked with me to join our magic together."

This time, the wizard snorted. "My goodness!" He visibly tried to calm himself. "I suspected it was so, but my mind would not believe it. You are certainly no elf. I do not understand how you could possibly communicate with it, let alone link." He paused, giving the boy an appraising look. "Then again, we have never had a human display the Red Level of magic. Perhaps your Power allows such a connection. The elves can connect with dragons naturally. They are different from humans in that they are all born with the Power and are the only race where their magic is the colour of their eyes."

"So, a blue-eyed elf is at the Blue Level of magic?" asked Eleanor.

"Yes. Green-eyed elves are Green Level mages, and so on," the wizard answered. "Humans have different-coloured eyes that do not necessarily match their Power Level. Chip has green eyes but Red Level magic. You are definitely human, boy. You cannot be elven since your eyes do not match your Level. You also do not have pointed ears." He squinted at him. "Then again, your eyes were red at birth. You are also an orphan, so your lineage ..." He shook himself. "Well, no use conjecturing."

"So why is it not a normal egg?" Chip asked before Chase figured out the wizard had not answered his original question.

"Ah, yes. I was getting to that," Xander remembered with a nod. "I was born after the last Elf War, right before the Great Battle. I never had the privilege of seeing a dragon until recently in front of the gates of Vanalon. They were supposed to be extinct. Growing up, I had many talks with the Light Elves in the Wizard's Guild. Elf King

Luminor would sit with me, sharing stories of magic and dragons. I sat mesmerized, listening to his musical voice describing the great battles of the Elf Wars over the centuries. I asked him many questions about dragons as boys do, and he told me many things." He looked again in wonder at the egg. "The King of the Light Elves said nobody knows what happened before the Great Forget, but the legends say two dragons appeared after the skies settled down. Historically, that would place their appearance about two millennia before the Great Battle, one millennium before the Breaking. One black dragon and one white dragon, male and female, appeared. These two dragons laid a dozen perfect eggs, six black and six white. According to the histories, both dragons died shortly after fulfilling their purpose.

"Those twelve eggs were deemed the Originals. The elves swear they felt a calling when the eggs birthed but could not determine the source. The trolls discovered the eggs high in the mountains hundreds of years later and returned with them to their fortress. But they never hatched. At the time, the elves and trolls had an uneasy alliance. They had fought for centuries before to determine boundaries after the Great Forget. In the end, the trolls held the north, and the elves settled south where Toron now stands."

"The capital used to be under elven control?" asked Chase in wonder. Princess Eleanor gave him an amused look. Chip tried not to grin, knowing his friend had not paid attention to Miss Owl's history lectures.

"Yes," the wizard answered. "Below Toron sits the remnants of the old elvish city of Tarana, which sits above the Ancient City of the Red-Eyed King."

"Why would the elves leave?" asked Chase with a puzzled look.

"I will tell you if you let me finish," Xander scolded, though it was light-hearted. Both boys gave an eager nod. It was clear they wanted to hear more about dragons. The wizard took a long drink from his water skin. "In the second last battle with the trolls, before they settled their lands, King Luminor's father had succumbed to grievous injuries from a duel with the Troll King Malkor. The elves were at risk of extinction. Luminor took the crown off his dead father's head, placed it on his own, and strode forward in vengeance. Though he could not defeat the trolls, he fought them to a stalemate, at which point Malkor agreed to an uneasy alliance. Some say he feared King Luminor's Power and did not wish to test him, though he was a formidable mage. Luminor desperately wanted to avenge his father, but the elves were few, so he agreed to a truce. His honour forbade him from violating the new agreement. The elves settled in Tarana, and the trolls held the north.

"Many years passed in an uneasy peace, but the elves still felt the pull of the eggs created when the Original Twelve were birthed. However, they could not determine the source of this connection, and the centuries passed. One day, Troll King Malkor, father to the current King Jaggar, threw a fit and smashed some of the eggs hidden in his fortress. It took great physical and magical strength to break them, but half were destroyed before he needed rest. The elves, one race at the time before the Breaking, felt a distant pain in their hearts after each egg broke and decided to journey to the source to investigate. This time, they could pinpoint the location of the pull as it had grown in strength, likely due to the Troll King's actions. Malkor, exhausted, threw the rest of the eggs inside one of his dungeons to rot.

"The elves arrived at Rathgar, the troll capital fortress, several weeks later to the surprise of King Malkor, who hurried to the gates with arms folded. He stood ready with his guards in case the elves tried to violate the truce. Instead, they asked him if he had wielded great magic several weeks before as they felt a disturbance. He told them he had destroyed a few odd eggs that some troll wanderers had found centuries before in the mountains, which never hatched.

"King Luminor asked if he could see the remains of the eggs, so King Malkor offered him the ones that were not broken, as he had no use for them. He sent servants to retrieve the eggs while the elves waited uncomfortably outside the gates. When the servants returned, the Troll King opened the gates only enough to send a small company of guards out to deliver the eggs.

"They set down a large basket before King Luminor, who gazed at the six perfect remaining eggs, four black and two white. The Elf King gasped, feeling a strong connection. Malkor was cunning and saw Luminor's reaction. He suddenly realized the value of the eggs to his elven enemies and called out for his soldiers to return them. King Luminor immediately had his Elven Guard surround the company of trolls. The Troll King screamed that the truce was broken even though, in Luminor's eyes, he only held Malkor true to his word to release the eggs. A fierce battle ensued, and King Luminor slew Malkor at the gates of Rathgar, finally avenging his father. The elves though were still outnumbered and forced to retreat. Jaggar, Malkor's son, placed the troll crown of stone on his head, vowing vengeance. The egg basket overturned in the melee, and the elves could only retrieve three of the six."

Chip did a quick calculation, then smiled. "They got two black and one white." Chase looked at him perplexed, trying to decipher how he arrived at that combination.

"Yes," the wizard said in appreciation. "That is the most the elves could have received. The other two black eggs and the remaining white one, lost in the melee, ended up in the Demon King's possession. Two of them found their way here under Cave Mountain. How the Unnamed One received them remains a mystery. I am sure King Jaggar could shed some light on it, though he denied taking them during the battle in later years, instead proclaiming the three eggs lost. That leaves one missing black egg that the Demon King must have taken with him to Demon Island before we raised the barrier, hatching the black dragon Fang, which you slew in front of the gates of Vanalon." Chase screwed his face in a knot, trying to work out the numbers, then gave up. The princess nodded at the math.

The wizard carried on. "After King Luminor slew Malkor and took the three eggs, the elves retreated to Tarana, but the insult ignited a vicious series of battles between trolls and elves called the Retribution Wars. Every foot of ground was fiercely contested, and when both sides had dwindled, the race of humans swept in and pushed them all back. The trolls retreated far to the north and the elves east, where they built the beautiful white city of Elvar on the immense island of Lavralor. Tarana was destroyed in the battle between elves and men, and Toron was built later on its ashes."

"Why did the elves not use the eggs to hatch dragons and destroy the trolls? And the humans, for that matter?" Eleanor asked, enraptured by the story.

"Ha. Good question. The answer is the dragons would not hatch. They birth themselves when ready. Only the elves can make the conditions right for birth, but it is apparently dragons themselves that choose when to emerge. King Luminor admitted in one of our talks when I was a boy that it took the elves centuries to figure out how to get the conditions right. I think it was likely a combination of the two: the right conditions and the willingness of the dragons. In any event, hundreds of years passed, and peace settled over the lands. King Luminor was weary of rule and passed the crown to his younger brother Galal, who had a son named ..." He paused, then looked up. "I suppose saying the name for now will do little harm. We already announced our presence when you brought down half of Cave Mountain. Galal's son is Prince Killian, now the Demon King."

Chase whistled, and the princess's eyes widened. Xander looked around warily then carried on. "It was during this time that the first dragons decided to emerge from their hard shells. The elves learned how to nurture the babies to adulthood and then ride them. All three eggs hatched, two males and one female. Their Power was unmatched. They were the Originals. Interestingly, the dragons chose their elvish riders, not the other way around."

"How do they choose?" Chip interrupted. He sensed amusement from the egg.

"They bend a knee."

Chip blinked. "Come again."

The wizard laughed. "They bow down, showing loyalty to their rider, accepting them as master. Luminor could not decide if they were bound by their master or chose to listen." The amusement in the egg increased. Chip felt the corners of his lips twitch. Xander looked at him oddly. "He did say the black dragons were more aggressive and stronger in the Power." Outright laughter suddenly spewed from the egg, causing Chip to laugh out loud inadvertently. The wizard stared, and Garth even arched an eyebrow. "What is so funny?"

"The egg is laughing at you." Chip held out his hand, trying to let his mirth subside. Xander's eyes widened. "It is showing me an image of a white dragon laughing. I can feel it when she finds things funny."

Xander looked surprised, then finally amused. "My goodness. I guess maybe she should tell the story."

Chip started laughing all over again, but then a series of images entered his mind. The first showed Elf King Galal, Luminor's brother, raising dragons and their babies until several dozen had been born.

"What is it?" asked Eleanor, following the different expressions on his face.

"It... I mean she, is showing me the elves raising dragons and ..." He paused, his face slowly darkening.

"What do you see?" the princess asked, squeezing his hand.

He did not answer then finally dropped his head. After several moments, he looked up at them. "She showed me the Breaking. Morgo taught the young elf Prince Killian how to bring down his Wall. The Power corrupted him, and his eyes went black. He then slew his father, King Galal, and took the black dragons with him when he fled the city with his followers. The elves separated into two factions, Light and Dark. Luminor assumed the crown again after his brother's death. The fiercely loyal dragons fought for their riders until almost none were left." He paused, seeing a final memory and looked up with sadness. "She showed me the death of the last white dragon."

Xander said nothing as he studied the boy. For once, even the wizard was stumped. "How is that possible?"

Chip closed his eyes as she showed him the answer and opened them in shock. He looked at the egg then all of them with wonder. "Any descendants of the Original dragons were weaker. Some could not even breathe fire. The more dragons that were born, the more their magic spread out. It was as if the Original dragons had a finite amount of Power for their race. Yet it works in reverse too. As each dragon dies, the Power intensifies in those that remain."

Xander's eyes widened. "Now there are only two."

"Yes," Chip answered. "Only two of the twelve Originals remain." He pointed at the egg. "She is one of them."

They all looked in amazement at the white egg, trying to imagine the immense Power that had intensified in the final two dragons.

"But what about her memories?" asked Xander. "Could it be …"

"Yes. She has all the memories of all the white dragons that existed. Their Power is concentrated in her."

"That means that the black egg …"

"Has all the memories and Power of the black dragons," Chip finished. "The black egg buried under Cave Mountain has the memory of me destroying the last black dragon, Fang. No wonder it sent me feelings of hostility. One more thing: the black dragons are not more powerful. They are simply males and more prone to aggression, which gives the impression they are stronger. Their nature and need for dominance make them more susceptible to the use of force. Unfortunately, the lone black egg now has the memories of all the evil actions the black dragons have committed over the centuries. It now fully believes in the cause of the Demon King. In essence, it is now evil."

He felt a sense of satisfaction from the white egg.

"Darn," Chase interjected. "We should have destroyed it when we had the chance."

Chip paused as the egg showed him several more images. "She says there is a balance in life. Right now, it is off, and the Dim is the correction. The Great Forget created the imbalance in the first place. It might not be a coincidence that the Dim appeared on the small island under Cave Mountain right before we could retrieve the black egg. We were never meant to hold it. She believes we determine our fate, but some things are beyond our control. They are meant to be. She is happy that, at least for now, the black egg is buried under half a mountain.

"The magic used in the Great Forget created a massive imbalance that has not been rectified. The problem with correcting these imbalances, such as the Dim, is that they may overcorrect and wipe out everything. These imbalances can allow one side to subjugate the other and even eradicate them. The Demon King could be the sole survivor of a lifeless world, riding a black dragon alone over the dead Earth. She says we must stop him, or all will be lost."

Silence fell over them as they pondered her words. A cloud obscured the sun, dampening their spirits, but then it passed. They looked again upon the green grass, listening to the gentle gurgle of water, and felt the warm sunlight. Finally, the companions lifted their heads with a renewed purpose, knowing they needed to stop the Demon King and restore the balance.

"So where do we begin?" asked Chase cheerily.

Chip waited as he received a final slew of images. "She says her Power has been strained by helping me bring down Cave Mountain. It is highly unusual for her to attempt such a feat in her egg state, but she believes these are the end of times and that the old ways must change. Even so, the chances of us surviving this are small. The Paths are becoming fewer. Yet, there is still hope. She believes nobody, not even the Creator himself, can take away free will. Most Paths now lead to the death of humankind, some to the end of everything. The Dim eats the Paths." They all sat straighter, remembering what young Han had said. "The dragons believe in the Balance. The Dim is the extreme manifestation of imbalance.

"Yet so are the dragons. They may be the balance to the Dim. Whoever unleashed the Great Forget could not have foreseen these consequences and for that reason is not the Creator. They exercised free will, whether man, elf, or something else. A magic of unimaginable magnitude was released in the distant past, causing a chain reaction.

"The Dim is trapped under the mountain for now. Know that the Age of Dragons is not over. They still have a role to play. The races must work together or perish. The Demon King is the greatest threat to life and does not understand what he has unleashed. All will be lost if we stray or take the wrong path. We must ally ourselves. Follow the son of Arkan to the Guild and build an army. She must go into a long sleep to regain her strength. She will not be available until a time of her choosing. Stay alert, for a new Path has opened... Danger is coming...something is following... Fare well."

The images stopped. Any connection to the egg disappeared.

Chip looked at them. "She is gone now. I recommend we bathe in this wonderful stream and then try to reach the foothills before sunset. I, for one, need a good night's sleep." The boy stood up and stretched. The enormity of all that had happened washed over him. He looked again at the egg in wonder. Now he knew why her Power was so strong.

"I second that," said Chase. "I still feel those nasty spider webs on me from Fang Forest." He scratched his arms and shuddered while the others laughed. Within seconds, Chase disrobed almost completely, but at the last moment, he realized the princess was still there and kept his small clothes on. With a whoop, he leapt into the river, which was only waist high. Garth threw him a bar of soap from a pouch at his waist. Eleanor laughed and retrieved several items from her travel bag before moving further downstream around a bend in the river behind a cluster of trees. The others took turns, as there was only one bar of soap.

Afterwards, they all felt refreshed enough to continue their journey. The last two days had taken a steep toll on them, the least of which was the dark circles under their eyes, but the feeling of not being hunted, however fleeting, buoyed their spirits. This was overshadowed by the dragon's cryptic words before she fell into her deep sleep.

"Something is following."

3

The companions walked until they reached the first of a series of foothills leading to the Great Plains. The sun was setting, so they built a makeshift camp using cedar branches for shelter and a small fire. It was a risk they were willing to take. Garth left to return an hour later with two small hares dangling from a hook around his waist. Dusk approached as he set about skinning the rabbits. They had started a fire as soon as he left, so the coals were glowing bright orange when he returned. None of them had eaten an authentic meal since the Oak Inn in the hamlet of Forest Glen.

"Rabbit again?" Chase said in disbelief and then saw Garth's glower. "Not that I'm complaining, of course." He smiled weakly.

The weapons master threw a few flat rocks on the coals, which turned piping hot. He expertly strung pieces of meat along a few thin, young branches that would not burn too fast and laid them out on the hot rocks. A satisfying sizzle sounded, and the smell of roasting meat made everyone's mouth water. While turning the sticks, Garth added a few spices, which Xander provided. After a while, he examined his handiwork and gave each of them a rod.

The companions devoured the crispy, succulent, steaming meat between cold gulps of river water. The process repeated for the second rabbit.

Amidst the satisfied smiles and finger-licking, even Chase had to admit it was delicious. "If rabbit always tasted like that, I could eat it every day," he said, leaning back with an indulgent smile.

The wizard concurred, pulling out his pipe. "I cannot argue the point."

They watched as the old man took a pinch of tobacco from a small pouch that never seemed to empty, then stuffed his pipe. Lighting it with his finger, he gave them a wink and took a long pull. When he exhaled, wide concentric rings floated lazily into the night.

"What does that taste like?" Chase asked curiously.

"Try some," offered the wizard, handing him the pipe. Chase took it in surprise, then looked at it suspiciously. Finally, he shrugged and took a deep pull. Chip noticed Garth trying to hide a rare smile. There was a moment when Chase seemed to enjoy the experience, but he made the mistake of inhaling too deep. To his credit, he maintained a stoic expression as his face went purple for a reasonable period of time, until he started coughing violently like a dying dragon.

Pathetic puffs of smoke escaped his nostrils at various intervals when he was not doubled over trying to gasp for air. Xander watched with great amusement, winking at the weapons master while reaching for another piece of rabbit. Chip had to point and laugh.

Finally, when he could speak, Chase shrieked, "How can you stand that?"

The wizard chuckled, taking the pipe back as the boy thrust it at him as if it were a venomous snake. "I have to admit it does take some getting used to." Xander took a deep pull and sat back with a contented smile. Chase shook his head in disbelief. Chip wiped his eyes and then stretched. A wave of weariness washed over him. The wizard gave him a knowing look. "Rest now, young man. You have earned it. We will wake you for watch last."

The boy nodded at the wizard and then looked at Eleanor with bleary eyes.

"I will retire as well," she said, yawning. Chip caught her glancing at him as he turned and hid a smile. "I bid you good night." They all bowed their heads in acknowledgement to the princess as the two of them walked to the makeshift shelter and slid under the long pine branches propped at an angle against a large, oblong stone. The others continued with small talk. They could hear Chase complaining that his chest was sore and felt like it would never stop burning. Chip bunched his cloak under his head in the darkness and settled down.

He felt the princess snuggle up beside him. The boy arranged his cloak so both could rest their heads on it while she draped her beautiful silk robe over their bodies. He glimpsed some stars through the end of the structure, but otherwise, it was almost pitch black. Soft shadows danced across the side of the rock from the dancing flames of the dying fire. Eleanor moved closer to him, and he inhaled the heady smell of her floral soap.

"I was so worried about you today," she murmured sleepily, then leaned in and kissed his cheek. He instinctively put his arm under her head, which she rested on his shoulder.

"Same," he said and kissed her forehead. She hugged him tighter. He wanted to talk more and kiss her again but was only able to mumble something as an immense weariness enveloped him. He tried to stay up but could not keep his eyes open. He heard her giggle and snuggle closer. His last thought was how peaceful he felt at that moment, and then a wave of darkness washed over him.

Sometime later, Chip vaguely heard Chase blunder into the shelter like a bear and crash beside them, snoring within moments.

XANDER SAT with the weapons master, still enjoying his pipe. He let out a long smoke ring and then blew several smaller ones through it. The fire crackled, with the occasional light pop sending sparks through the night air. He waited a while until he was sure everyone was asleep, then looked at his Protector.

"He is the one."

"It only took you three millennia to find him," Garth said with a small smile.

"True, but at least we have a chance now. The boy has fulfilled another part of the prophecy. He is the only human to link with a dragon, as was foretold. I could not believe my eyes. No one without the Orb of Power has ever displayed such a feat of magic. He knocked half the mountain down, and that's when he was drained!" the wizard whispered in disbelief.

"The egg helped," Garth added.

"The dragon will be a great asset if we can find the Light Elves to birth her."

"Indeed."

The wizard took another pull on his pipe. "I am concerned Killian might sense a display of magic of that magnitude. My goodness, they may even have felt it at the Guild." He smiled.

Garth nodded. "There is nothing we can do about that. Let us assume he sensed it and sent out trackers, even assassins. We must be wary and make haste to the Guild."

Xander agreed. "We will resupply in Banfar. We have no choice. The dwarf magician Scar may wish to have a word." He grimaced. "Let us try not to make a fuss this time, shall we?" He glanced at the weapons master with a pained look.

"I should be able to control myself," Garth responded shortly before changing the subject. "When we reach the Guild, Skylar will want to see him."

The wizard sighed. "Yes, he undoubtedly will. The fool will try to control him by making decisions based on the vague understanding of the Tellings, likely causing the prophecy he's trying to predict, and then pat himself on the back for his accuracy."

"Occasionally, he is right."

"Agreed, but the risk of a miscalculation at these end times is great. A mistake could be catastrophic. My brother puts great faith in him, which I feel is largely misplaced. Prophecy can be interpreted in many ways, depending on the reader's motive. It is partly the reason we left in the first place. Balor is a slave to his need to control the destiny of others." The wizard looked at Garth. "He will try and use the boy."

"Yes. As will others. The need to control is part of the human condition. Most never recognize it. Chip is young and must learn. We will guide him as best we can."

The wizard nodded and looked deep into the fire. "Finding the egg eliminates many Paths. The linking narrows it further. Han's foretelling came true." A look of sadness crossed Xander's face as he thought about another prophecy.

"You know what will happen if you tell him," Garth looked over at his long-time friend, acknowledging his pain.

"He should know," the wizard said, wringing his hands.

"If any human utters a word to him, the very telling of it will cause the prophecy to unravel, and all is lost. You know this," Garth said softly.

Xander nodded, eyes wet. "I know, yet maybe it is not true."

"If that is the case, then telling him will not matter anyway."

The wizard sighed, looking at his Protector. "Well said, old friend."

Garth glanced at the tent. "Let them enjoy what time they have left."

Xander leaned back, looking at the stars. "Dear Creator, I hope it shall not pass." He made a silent prayer and then looked up. "All we can do in this life is cherish what we have now. Let us do so with a light heart. We ride on a wave of victory, however temporary it may be. Let us not fret over things we cannot control. Prophecy cannot account for free will. I will always believe that. Let me take the first watch, no arguments. I will wake you when it is time. I think tonight we let them sleep. They carried a greater burden than us."

The weapons master nodded. "What about Chase?"

"My goodness, he should be punished for asking silly questions. I will wake him next." They both chuckled. Garth put his hand on the wizard's shoulder for a moment then found a spot under the shelter.

The wizard gazed into the fire for a long time. Everything he had strived towards for three thousand years was coming to a head. He had worked tirelessly, many times following false leads. Yet, finally, he had found the one.

He remembered reading Queen Charlotte's message almost sixteen years ago. It was not the first time someone had claimed a baby had been born with red eyes. Yet it was the first from her, and he knew from her training at the Wizard's Guild that the queen's judgment was sound. In a leap of faith, he moved with his Protector to Vanalon. His decision rested on a hunch and growing disagreements with his brother Balor. They were at odds on a number of issues, from the training of students to relationships with the races to the meaning of prophecy.

Xander had always been the voice of reason to his brother's need for control. Balor had fractured the council three millennia ago when he assumed control without a vote. Jaggar, the Troll King, felt he was more capable and should be High Mage.

When Jaggar attacked the Wizard's Guild with his troll army, Xander and Balor had no choice but to flee. They had rebuilt the Guild a day's ride north of Toron. It was much further south than the original but better located. His brother had paid for the construction with chests of gold he had removed from the old Guild and then maintained it by a tithe he charged to the human cities. In return, he provided counsel, training for those displaying magical abilities, and protection. The amount of the tax and how he demanded it was a bone of contention between them.

The old wizard shook his head. He much preferred simpler times. Xander looked west towards the mountains and the growing threat. He knew the Demon King would respond quickly to the boy's use of magic. Chip had needed to use it, but it would trigger a chain of events. Hopefully, Killian would pause to dig out the black egg. His longing to ride the last black dragon unchallenged through the skies would likely outweigh his decision to press forward and secure victory. His greed and need for power should buy them precious time to mount a proper defence.

The Dim was another matter entirely. The Demon King would find out immediately that he could not control it anymore. He was cunning though and would still try to use the creature to his advantage. He could try to contain it with his magic and unleash it at will on any city by simply throwing it over the walls and then letting the creature do its work. With great luck, Killian would become careless, and the Dim would touch him, ending their greatest threat, yet Xander knew not to believe in fairy tales. The Demon King was evil and consumed by his need for more power, but he was no fool. He would recognize the threat the Dim posed and use the creature carefully to do his bidding. The Power Killian must possess after feeding off others for three millennia terrified the wizard.

As strong as the boy was, even in combination with the white dragon, he would likely pale before the Unnamed One.

The old man sighed. The truth was they stood little chance. Many old, powerful wizards, magicians, and mages were dead and gone. Even three millennia ago, with the aid of the Orb of Power, they could not defeat the Demon King. They barely managed to contain him, which was only achieved by his father and several other great wizards sacrificing their spirit essences. Xander bent his neck in weariness. A hurricane was coming towards them, and they were holding a candle.

Hope remained, though faint. He believed in the Creator and the Balance, even against impossible odds. Xander's faith gave him the strength to carry on. A stark realization struck him. Whoever won this war would likely gain the knowledge of the Great Forget. He suspected that knowledge would be more helpful in preventing or turning the tide of the war in the first place. For now, it was hidden.

Xander yearned for that knowledge. Balor and Killian lusted for power. His need was for knowledge and learning. For him, knowledge advanced the world, not control. In fact, too much control stifled knowledge. It was learning that mattered, or else what was the point?

He remembered young Han and Chip sharing what they believed was an inside joke about silver hair. He had played it off at the time. The wizard looked at the stars in the sky and thought of the man with the silver hair. If he was involved, then indeed, it was the end of times.

Xander shook his head in wonder, remembering his own experience all those millennia ago. Not even Garth knew. No one did. One day, he would tell the boy. The wizard would know when the time was right. After all, the man with the silver hair had said so.

4

Chip woke from a warm cocoon of bliss. His eyes fluttered in the bright sunlight as he fought the waking reality of life. The boy's training kicked in, and he heard the weapons master's voice say he had no choice but to get up. Life was easy for him when his brain knew it had no choice. It stopped trying to trick or tempt him and followed orders. He threw off the last tendrils of sleep and opened his eyes wide. Staring back at him were the princess's beautiful, bright-blue irises.

She giggled at his startled look then hugged him impulsively.

"Wake up, sleepy head." He realized they were still entwined under the cedar branches. The brightness of the light coming through the makeshift shelter could only mean it was well into the morning.

"I think we slept half the day away," he laughed, not letting her go.

He felt her giggle again. "I have been up for the last hour but did not want to wake you. You looked so peaceful."

A head appeared around the corner of the shelter.

"Well, it's about time," Chase chastised, trying to look stern. He noticed they were still holding each other and rolled his eyes. "If you two lovebirds are done with your beauty sleep, would you care to join us for lunch?"

"Lunch!" Chip exclaimed. He extricated himself from the princess and sat up in shock. "That is the longest I have ever slept." He suddenly felt a voracious hunger.

"You needed it." Eleanor patted his hand. She then looked over at Chase, who was trying not to laugh. "And that is no way to talk to a princess, young man," she said with mock indignation.

"Well, it's true, Your Highness. Now get up before I drag you out, princess or not." He was gone before she could call out his insolence and lecture him on the chain of command. She laughed and pushed Chip down as he tried to get up.

"Ow," he complained, then managed to snag her ankle as she scrambled out ahead of him.

"Me first," he said, pulling her backwards and then crawling over her as she tried to resist. He managed to get half his body out before she clasped him around the waist with both arms and flipped him sideways. This caused the entire shelter to collapse, covering them both with cedar branches. They cried out as the needles pierced their skin but managed to extricate themselves with only a few minor scratches. They grinned at one another, noticing bits of pine stuck in each other's hair, then turned towards the fire, both looking quite dishevelled.

Xander, Chase, and Garth stared at them wide-eyed. No one said a word. Chip and Eleanor looked back at each other at the same time, trying not to laugh. Chase rolled his eyes again while the Weapons Master pretended to study a beetle walking near the fire. Xander held a mild look of amusement, then pretended they were not standing in the middle of a small mountain of cedar branches in the destroyed shelter. "Ah, there you are. Lunch, anyone?"

"Yes," the princess said in delight, using Chip's shoulder as leverage to leap over several branches and approach the fire. He followed as best he could, taking high steps to press down on the pesky needles so they would not scratch him further.

Five small quail sizzled on hot rocks over the coals, and a pouch of freshly picked berries stood open beside the fire pit. They picked up their water skins and drank their fill before passing around the bag of berries. Garth removed the plump birds from the fire to cool them, and a short while later, they tore with vigour into the crispy skin and juicy meat. Chip did not bother asking the weapons master how he caught the tasty fowl but instead savoured the meal.

Garth was a man of many talents who could cook with the best. Miss Stern would have found him a welcome kitchen addition if he had applied. The boy then realized the personality clash and thought it was much better he did not.

The companions all ate the delicious meal while making small talk and commenting on the beautiful, warm autumn weather.

"Let's pack up. It's getting late," the wizard said when everyone finished. He noticed the guilty look on the faces of Chip and the princess. "Do not worry. Your rest was well deserved. If we leave now, we can reach the plains by midafternoon. We will camp between the foothills and the Witch Town of Banfar tonight and enter the gates tomorrow afternoon."

"Why is it called the Witch Town," Chase asked.

The wizard looked at him as if it was obvious. "Well, for one, there used to be a disproportionate number of witches there. Most were charlatans and cult members, but a few were actual Seers with some predictive capabilities. Banfar was founded three millennia ago at the end of the Great Battle. The Demon King had a small following of humans who believed in his cause. They formed a cult to worship him a two-day ride east of Cave Mountain, believing he would rise again.

"These dangerous groups were driven underground over the centuries as the various High Kings of Toron banned them, with only partial success. Though evidence is scant, most witches settled much further north near the Secret Caves. The High Kings did not strictly enforce the ban unless certain zealots drew attention to themselves.

"Several centuries ago, the town was almost razed to the ground when the capital found out the majority of townsfolk had joined the cults. Some were sacrificing babies to a horned statue of the Demon

King. When asked why the Unnamed One would spare them upon his return, they claimed he would recognize their devotion and honour them with positions of power over the human slaves.

"Since then, a sizable group of fanatics continue to practice underground, but they are relatively harmless. However, given recent events, I expect a resurgence of the cults. I am certain that news of the falling barrier and the attack by the demon army on Vanalon has reached Banfar. I frankly do not know what to expect. Witches, outsiders, drug addicts, con artists, and those on the fringes of society have tended to congregate in this town. Even though it is part of Amrika, the soldiers from Toron only make sporadic visits to this distant city, usually to sabre rattle or knock a few heads to keep people in line. A small contingent of guards is stationed in Banfar, but they are bribed to keep quiet about nefarious affairs. In the last couple decades or so, a dwarf mage named Scar has taken over the city, apparently with the blessing of the commander in Toron. I would like to avoid him." The wizard glanced at Garth. "Keep your wits about you. The town is full of prostitutes, pickpockets, conmen, and charlatans."

"Great," said Chase with a grin. "Sounds like a fun place."

Eleanor elbowed him, and he feigned injury. They left the makeshift camp a short while later, walking steadily. Chip used the time to look at his surroundings. They were traversing low foothills that would eventually give way to flat ground. In between the hills were lush meadows full of autumn butterflies. The leaves on most of the trees were already beginning to turn gold and red in anticipation of the coming winter. The sun was bright and strong, a welcome respite from the dark confines of the caves. He breathed deeply, smelling the rich mountain air.

The boy held the princess's hand, making small talk as they walked, sometimes stopping to look at a rocky formation or even a strange insect. He had never been this far from home in his life, excluding his unknown origins. He wondered where he may have come from for the thousandth time and why his parents had abandoned him. Likely the eyes, he thought with sadness.

It would have been nice to know them. He looked at his companions, realizing with a start that if his real parents had raised him, he would not have met his friends. Garth's voice entered his head from his training, reminding him to 'always be grateful' for what he did have. No matter how difficult life could and would become, he remembered there was always something to be grateful for.

He tried to abide by that belief. Even when life sent him rotten apples, he tried to welcome the chance to learn from that experience. "We only learn when we are uncomfortable," repeated the weapons master in his mind. Chip laughed inwardly at how one lesson usually led to another.

The boy had learned that all misery eventually passed. Nothing stayed the same forever. For now, he would relish the challenges put before him. He already had succeeded where most thought he would fail and learned much on the journey. The road ahead would be difficult, but he would consider it an adventure. So far, it was much harder than he would have liked but very rewarding.

Chip looked sideways at the princess. Her beauty made his heart flutter. With her next to him, he knew nothing could stop them. For a moment, he thought of what life would be like without her, and a vast chasm opened before him. He shoved the thought aside, vowing to ensure he never lost her. The alternative was not something he cared to contemplate.

She caught his stare and smiled. The boy's face lit up, and he pulled her down the hill, forcing her to run to keep up with him until both had trouble slowing down, causing further laughter.

The afternoon stretched on, and the sun's rays began to slant. The foothills became smaller until, finally, they arrived in front of a field of wheat.

Chip gaped in awe at the endless flatness of it all. It was the biggest field he had ever seen, stretching all the way to the eastern horizon. He turned back to see Cave Mountain far in the distance.

Eleanor watched him and smiled, commenting on the mountain's new shape. "It looks old and worn, like a witch's hat or a bent old man. When the Demon King sees what you did to his mountain, he will not be happy."

"No, I would imagine not. I'm hoping it will take him a while to dig out the Dim and the egg."

"Let's hope he won't know the Dim's whereabouts," interjected Xander, arriving beside them. "Leaving it buried is the best solution for everyone."

"He will know," Chip said with a sigh. "I felt the Dim's absence with my magic. Its very non-existence makes it stand out. He may be in for a surprise when it reaches for him though."

The wizard nodded. "I fear his Power will still be able to cage and direct it, or at least point it towards humans. If he threw it over the walls of a city, he could likely sit back and wait until everyone dies. Then, of course, there is the matter of the egg. The Unnamed One linked to the magic of the last black dragon is terrifying."

"I will find the Orb of Power," Chip said. "We need to bring the Light Elves the dragon egg anyway. Do you think they would go for a trade?" He looked at the wizard with a glint of amusement in his eyes.

Xander laughed. "It is worth a try." Chip patted the pouch by his side, holding the egg. The white dragon had been entirely silent since she went into the long sleep. He wished he had asked her how long these hibernation-type periods lasted, but it was too late now. He did not try to communicate with her because she made it clear she would not respond.

The companions turned back to the Great Plains and found a trail leading straight east, thanks to Garth. It was hard to imagine many people, besides the occasional hunter, going in this direction. According to Xander, Banfar traded most of their goods with Calgar and Toron. Given the almost endless supply of wheat, they could trade the crop for anything they needed from the other cities.

"Let us walk until late evening today," the wizard said. "I am not concerned about the terrain. There are no holes, roots, or trees to stumble on. The snakes are venomous but should slither off long before our arrival, unless you accidentally step on one. The moon will be quite bright tonight. There are few predators on the Great

Plains except for the occasional pack of prairie wolves and the charging buffalos. They will only charge if you stare them down and do not run. As long as they feel they own the land, they will leave you alone."

"So what happens if they charge?" asked Chase.

"You run," the wizard snapped. "Beyond that, the apex predator is the brown tiger, which uses the grass for camouflage. They are usually found further north. If you see one, it is likely too late. The beasts do not particularly like human flesh but will snatch an unsuspecting villager here and there if game is scarce. The tigers are so adept at killing they will give you a warning to make it more fun. Very few survive the encounter. We should be alright." He squared his shoulders and set off along the path between the endless rows of wheat.

Chase looked around at the others to see their reactions. The weapons master was already following without expression. The tall boy stood there exasperated, then shouted, "So what is the warning?"

Xander did not slow. "Oh. They growl first then pounce a few moments later."

Chase stared at him wide-eyed. "Great. I am so happy there's nothing to worry about." He followed along, mumbling to no one in particular. Chip and the princess shared a look and then smirked.

The orphan decided to use the time to try to appreciate the geography. The openness of it all felt strange to him. He had only ever known the mountains. There was something oddly protective about the valley he grew up in. Here, it was so open that he almost felt naked and fearful. It seemed plain wrong. He thought that was probably why they called it the "plains." He laughed inwardly, but something must have betrayed his expression, for the princess looked at him with raised eyebrows. He explained his play on words, and then she agreed.

"I never thought much of the plains either," she said, leaning in. "By the third week, you will give anything to see a single tree. The road from Calgar to Toron is similar, except it is much wider and small villages are common to make it more bearable. We will not have that luxury. I have never gone north to Banfar, because to be honest it is not a place for a princess."

He nodded. "For me, it would be interesting to see another city other than Vanalon. In the meantime, if you hear a growl, push Chase in front of you." They giggled, glancing at the taller boy, who gave them a suspicious look. That made them laugh harder. Chase finally rolled his eyes and continued mumbling to himself.

The path began to widen as they progressed. The late afternoon sun sunk behind them to the west. They looked back before it disappeared, marvelling at the fiery orange hue of the majestic sunset. Cave Mountain stuck out like a sore thumb within the Fang Mountain range, looking like a hideous, bent old man. Chip realized he had changed the landscape forever. It gave him hope that anything was possible.

Not long after, the sun disappeared, and the full moon appeared as a bright, perfectly round globe. The wind remained warm, and the sound of it brushing the top of the wheat stalks to either side was soothing. The party continued at a steady pace as the night enveloped them when suddenly the weapons master gave a sharp signal to the wizard.

They all stopped. Chip had no idea why but knew it must be important. He looked in the direction Garth was staring then saw it.

At first, only a single pair of eyes appeared, then another, until finally, he could see the moonlight glinting off a dozen. The eyes disappeared, then reappeared closer. Large wolf-like heads materialized over muscled shoulders. Slight rustles sounded behind him, and he whirled to see shapes skulking in the shadows. They were surrounded.

A mournful howl broke the silence, making the group jump. The animals surrounding them scattered into the night. "That howl did not come from a small prairie wolf," Garth whispered, "It was a mountain wolf. Judging by its tone, it is a rather large one. I do not know why it would range this far."

Chip felt the stir of several memories. "This is the third time I have heard its howl, always as a warning. When I began my Manhood Quest, I saw one tear apart a demon right before my eyes. Its howl woke me at base camp, right before the assassin demon attacked me. Even riding back to Vanalon, what looked like the same mountain wolf took out a demon as it leapt at me from a bush by the side of the road."

"There are stories of animal protectors throughout the ages," mused the wizard. "They are quite rare, but it is theoretically possible for a magic wielder to instruct an animal to protect a person. The problem, of course, is that few animals would care to listen. Remember the Cockadoo we flew in on to help you at the Pass of Death? We were lucky to get there alive." He paused and looked around. "Let me try something. I do not wish to reveal our location, but I believe this small risk is worth it." His eyes flared blue as he closed his eyes. Chip felt the peculiar crackle of magic. After several long moments, the wizard opened his eyes with a gasp. "I found it. A giant mountain wolf is watching half a league west. I will attempt some form of communication." He closed his eyes again, blue fire shining brightly behind his lids. "I have entered the wolf's mind." There was a long pause, and then Xander stopped and turned around with wide eyes. He stared at the boy.

"What is it?" asked Chip, betraying impatience.

The wizard's mouth worked. He finally found his voice. "This wolf has memories of you as a baby."

The boy stepped forward. "How is that possible?"

"I...do not know."

Chip grabbed the wizard's shoulders. "Did you see who held me when I was a baby?" His voice took on an earnest note.

"The wolf showed me an image of a baby with red eyes lying alone at the gates of Vanalon. I tried to look into its mind further, but it shut me out."

Chip stared for a moment longer, then his eyes blazed red, and he pushed past the wizard, walking west.

"Chip, don't!" shouted Xander. "It could be a trap."

Without slowing, the boy retorted, "It has saved my life and warned me many times. I will take that chance." He strode onward into the night. Even as he walked, the boy reached out with his Power, sensing the life forms in the area. He recognized the pack of prairie wolves now moving north, wanting no part of a much larger mountain wolf and human magic. They would not be back.

Chip sent his mind west and sensed the giant beast waiting for him. Its size was intimidating. He was apprehensive but felt no fear. His desire to know about his parents outweighed any risks. He was also confident in his Power. It filled him with a thrilling elixir of joy and strength. Chip had recovered from his ordeal in Cave Mountain and felt strong. The others tried to follow him, but he knew the wolf would feel threatened by too many humans. The boy turned around, eyes blazing, and instructed them to stay where they were. Garth nodded, and the others reluctantly agreed.

The orphan felt a surge of excitement that he might learn something about his heritage. As he moved along the path into the night, a warm wind sprang up over the wheat fields. The moonlight played off the tips of the stalks, giving them a shimmering quality. He ran his hands over the tops of the wheat as he walked forward, calming his mind. Finally, he began to make out the outline of the monstrous mountain wolf.

It sat impassively on its haunches, rising head and shoulders above the wheat, taller than he. It was gray, with a silver line running down the middle of its head. Massive, muscular shoulders bunched at his approach. The beast looked straight into his eyes and showed no fear. He stopped several feet from the animal and reached out with his magic.

The wolf allowed his presence to enter its mind. Chip immediately experienced non-human thoughts and a primitive, feral yearning to run free in the wild. The boy wrapped the wolf's awareness in the Calm to examine its memories. Even as he did, the beast threw the intrusion off. He realized the wild dog was cunning and that human Calm was not a soothing mechanism for it.

The creature could not be lulled into complacency or made to forget his presence. It was an apex predator that did not allow others to control it. The whole concept was foreign to its design. It lived for the hunt and thrill of catching prey. Deeply ingrained in its nature were the concepts of loyalty and honour, valuable virtues for mountain wolves hunting together in packs. Touching the creature's mind did show him that the packs had a hierarchy. Chip realized that this particular wolf was the leader of the Grey Mountains surrounding Vanalon. It was the King of the Mountain Wolves.

He re-entered the large animal's mind and waited patiently, respecting its boundaries. The wolf decided which memories it would allow him to see. Interestingly, the animal thought of him as a King of Humans. It was there when he fought the demons and the black dragon, watching from a distance.

The beast knew when it was wise to enter the fray or if its interference would make no difference. It showed him the memory of stalking the demon in the forest after the creature had disembowelled the fanged black bear during his Manhood Quest. The wolf knew the teeth and clawed demon would find the boy hiding behind the tree, so it intervened. The thrill of fighting another apex predator that could dispatch a black bear was irresistible.

When Chip faced the second demon on the bridge over the Rocky River, the wolf decided to allow the boy to test his skills, knowing the creature was beatable. The memory played out as Chip saw himself fight the demon and emerge victorious. The wolf could have intervened but looked at him as a human cub who needed to learn how to fight. Its respect for him grew as it watched the small human win against such a predator.

Another memory leapt into his mind of a small, cloaked demon climbing onto the cabin's roof at base camp and then sliding down the chimney. It was the assassin demon that almost killed him in his sleep. He saw the wolf run up to the cabin wall and let out a mournful howl, waking the boy in time to avoid certain death. The orphan then saw the beast watching him battle a dozen demons in front of the signal fire in the Pass of Death.

When Chip found and unleashed his magic, the wolf knew he was a Human King. The huge dog was going to assist the injured boy, but a large, awkward bird flew down to the pass carrying two humans who leapt off to save the child. After that, the dog watched from a distance as Chip and his two companions fell into a river. It felt concerned for the boy but could provide no help.

The mountain wolf picked up his trail downstream, then waited patiently for days outside the human city until it found his scent again. He watched the boy leave the gates of Vanalon with another tall human child on horses, heading to the villages. It had followed at a distance then sensed danger when a demon waited to ambush him as they returned from the human houses. It intercepted the creature as it pounced, saving Chip's life.

After that, it watched the demon army approach the gates, and a great battle ensued. When the black dragon emerged on the battlefield, even the mountain wolf shied away. It had never seen such a fearsome creature. Chip destroyed the winged beast with his magic, and the huge dog knew he was more powerful than all predators and deserved the utmost respect.

From there, the wolf lost his trail until he emerged from the escape tunnel on the outskirts of Vanalon. It smelled him on the wind and kept pace as the humans made their way down the One Road. It saw a large group of demons follow and then watched as the man in black took them on all by himself. Such was the beast's respect for this human's fighting ability that the wolf nearly stopped to help, but its mandate was to protect the boy, not the man in black.

After that, the wolf's memories jumped ahead to a group of assassin demons entering a barn, and Chip recognized the little village of Forest Glen. The loyal dog let out another howl to warn him of the attack, saving him again.

From there, the large animal kept pace in Fang Forest and watched as they entered Cave Mountain. It saw Zoran leading the Dim into the tunnel after them. When it saw the Dim, even the mountain wolf felt a wave of fear and disgust, for it sensed the creature's aberrant nature. It knew it had no power over such a thing, so the dog waited outside the entrance all night.

At dawn, something strange happened, and it felt the ground tremble as half the mountain caved in. The wolf could feel the air currents shift with the boy's magic and knew he had been victorious. It let out a howl of pure joy and raced around the mountain to find him. The huge dog found their tracks and followed the party down through the foothills to the plains, where it detected a pack of prairie wolves on the hunt. It knew that the small wolves were no match for him, but it feared the initial ambush might bring down the weakest in their party, so again, it let out a warning howl. Chip watched all this in wonder and thanked the great animal for its aid. The orphan then asked why it had helped him.

The mountain wolf paused, studying the boy for several long moments, and then a memory appeared of someone holding a baby wrapped in a blanket near the gates of Vanalon. The baby was still a distance away from the dog's location, but the moonlight revealed it had red eyes. Chip gasped. He looked at who was holding the baby, but a dark robe concealed the figure. He felt a sense of frustration but continued watching. The being strode up to the gates of Vanalon but stopped outside the torchlight to remain unseen by the guards.

The cloaked form started turning, and Chip's heart quickened as he waited to see the figure's face, but then it stopped. The being paused momentarily as it looked at the bundle in its arms and then leaned down to put the baby on the ground. Chip could not see the face, but as it bent down, a lock of silver hair fell out of its hood. The boy recoiled in shock. Could it be the man with the silver hair?

Then Chip noticed something else. As the figure put the baby on the ground, the being's sleeve pulled back, revealing a man's hand with a large blue ring. The man stood up and began walking away but stopped and paused, turning towards the mountain wolf. The light was behind him, so it was impossible to see his face. The cloaked figure began walking directly towards the animal.

The wolf sensed a level of confidence and power from the man and an unfamiliar scent. Its experience told it that this creature was very dangerous. The fact that it could sense the wolf was disturbing to the beast. It did not shy away from the man because it was the mountain wolf's territory, and here, it shied from no one. The outlines of a face began appearing. Chip held his breath. He could almost make out who it was. The face seemed familiar.

5

"Uh, just checking you are alright!" a voice called behind him. The mountain wolf pushed the boy out of its mind and growled menacingly. Chip turned around in shock to see Chase standing there, gawking at the sight of the massive animal.

"Is this a bad time?" he asked sheepishly. It took Chip all the control he had not to fling his friend into the wheat fields.

"Get out of here," the orphan managed between gritted teeth.

"Oh, so I guess you are fine then, right?" Chase asked in a timid voice.

"Yes, I'm fine!" Chip nearly screamed. The mountain wolf stood up, rippling with muscle, letting out a deep snarl. The moon glowed behind it, silhouetting its massive body.

Chase had fought many demons, but the wolf was as imposing a sight as he had likely ever seen. Its head almost reached his eye level, and he stepped back in surprise. "Uh, alright, so I'll be heading back now." He pointed his thumb behind him as he backed up. "Bye." The tall boy hurried away.

The wolf grunted and sat back down. Chip waited a moment, then carefully put his presence back into the animal's mind. The wolf sent him an image suggesting that Chase was a fearsome fighter but not very cunning. The orphan tried not to laugh while agreeing. Chip asked the wolf to replay its memory of him as a baby at the gates of Vanalon. An instant later, he was back looking through the wolf's eyes, reliving the memory of the figure approaching in the night. His heart sped up in anticipation.

The boy saw himself as a human baby lying on the ground in the distance, beginning to cry. The hackles on the animal raised in the memory as the cloaked form neared, and the wolf's muscles tensed in readiness to lunge. The unfamiliar scent became stronger as the figure approached. The outlines of the person's face started appearing in the moonlight. Chip could almost make out who it was. The wolf was about to leap.

Suddenly, the hooded figure's eyes blazed bright blue, revealing his face.

The orphan gasped in shock as he recognized who stood before the mountain wolf. He had seen him many times in Xander's memories. It was King Luminor. The King of the Light Elves froze the wolf with his Power as it flared to life. Luminor sent images into the majestic animal's mind, acknowledging it as a king, and then showed the animal what the future would hold.

He named the giant male wolf Silvermane in honour of his colouring. Images flashed of the future of the mountain wolves as the Lord of the Dark Elves destroyed the barrier and his demon army flooded the lands. The creatures spread out like ravenous beasts, eating everything in their wake. The wolves' food supply disappeared, and they were eventually slaughtered to the last.

Silvermane could tell the cloaked figure was telling the truth. The wolf knew this being was not a human by its scent. He was a king of a similar race called elves. The dog knew this future would be in the animal's lifetime. The wolf asked what the elf wished from it. Luminor asked if Silvermane would protect the baby, as the child would grow to be the only weapon against the coming darkness. The babe was the last hope of all the races.

Silvermane considered the future of its pack and even its prey and agreed to watch over the baby as he grew. The wolf gave its word, binding itself to the task until completion. The Elf King used no magic to force the wolf to obey, and it would not have worked on Silvermane anyway.

With that, the King of the Light Elves turned and was gone. The mountain wolf looked at the baby, crying in the cold. It trotted over to the little child and inhaled his scent, imprinting it on the wolf's memory for all time. It was a human baby. There was no elf in the child. Silvermane knew this by the boy's scent. Looking at the gates, the giant dog let out a mournful howl, causing the guards to look over and spy the small child. The mountain wolf trotted off, looking back once after the gates opened, and saw one of the guards bending down to pick up the tiny bundle. The soldier carried the crying baby inside the human city.

Silermane pulled back its memories and watched the boy with blazing red eyes. "Thank you," Chip sent a mental image. The wolf responded with an image of rending demons apart with its jaws, implying that that was thanks enough. The dog communicated that the mountains behind it were now under the control of Silvermane's son, who was even bigger.

The mountain wolf would accompany the boy until the demons were gone or it was defeated, whichever came first. Its honour forbade the beast to retract its oath. Silvermane's word was above all else. Besides, it was looking forward to hunting the brown tigers, who were formidable foes. Chip nodded, letting the fire go out of his eyes and releasing his Power.

HE STOOD as an ordinary boy in front of the great mountain wolf. He trusted it. Reaching out, Chip stepped forward and touched the magnificent silver hair, following it down the massive triangular head. Silvermane stared at the small human, knowing it could snap the orphan in two in one bite. The wolf, however, had no intentions of doing so, as it remained bound by its word. Moreover, the massive dog deeply respected the boy, acknowledging that he was the most dangerous predator the beast had ever seen. The orphan displayed the utmost trust and respect by standing defenceless before the King of the Mountain Wolves. Silvermane felt a loyalty to Chip reserved for its closest kin. Standing up, the giant animal bent its head in homage, then bounded away into the night.

THE BOY STOOD there for a while, digesting everything he had learned. He felt a connection to the wolf and a feeling of safety with a being that powerful watching over him.

The orphan finally turned to rejoin the others.

Chase was looking away with a guilty expression when he returned. Xander waited for the boy to speak, trying not to fidget. Chip looked deep in thought as he sat down amongst them. Garth watched in amusement.

Finally, the princess asked, "So, how did it go?" She looked at her nails, trying to appear disinterested. It was apparent she wanted to know who had dropped him off at the gates of Vanalon all those years ago.

"Oh, that," Chip said casually, trying not to laugh. The wizard looked incredulous. "Fine, but this is going to sound crazy." They all gathered around him. Even the weapons master showed curiosity. Chip didn't know where to begin, so finally, he blurted, "The mountain wolf saw who dropped me off at the gates of Vanalon when I was a baby." There was an indefinite pause as he looked at their shocked faces.

Finally, Xander could not take it anymore. "So, for goodness sake, who dropped you off?"

"King Luminor."

The wizard's knees almost buckled, and the weapons master had to grab his elbow. Princess Eleanor's eyes widened.

"You are an elf!" Chase said in disbelief. "That means you are related to the Unnamed One!"

Chip tried to follow the logic then rolled his eyes. "What? No, I'm not an elf. He only dropped me off."

Xander recovered and grabbed the orphan's ears to examine them. "Is it possible you have Luminor's elven blood in you?"

Chip laughed and pushed the wizard's hand away. "I assure you I have no elvish blood in me. Trust me, if I did, Silvermane would have smelled it."

"Silvermane?" said Garth, arching an eyebrow.

"Yes, King Luminor named the mountain wolf after he made him my protector." Even the weapons master showed a rare moment of surprise. Chip then recounted all of Silvermane's memories. When finished, Garth grunted.

Xander shook his head and slumped down on the path. "What on Earth was King Luminor doing in front of Vanalon sixteen summers ago? Where are the rest of the Light Elves? Where did he find you in the first place? And who are your real parents?" The wizard threw up his hands. "My goodness, there are more questions than answers." He pulled out his pipe and began muttering to himself.

"There are always more questions. I suppose that's life," Eleanor said, looking at Chip. "Want to go for a walk?" He nodded emphatically, happy to escape more questions. "Good. We can go in this direction where the land is flat for...ever, or we can try this opposite direction where, well, it's the same thing."

"Oh my," Chip said, pretending to think very hard. "Alright, I choose this way." He pointed down the path at the endless wheat fields. Chase looked at them as if they had three heads.

The princess grabbed his hand, and they ambled off into the night.

"I have more questions, but fine. Watch for prairie wolves," Xander called after them.

"They are all gone," Chip responded. "Don't worry. I'm well protected." He winked at Eleanor, and they walked out of earshot.

The full moon lit the path brightly over the glistening fields, and the sky sparkled with the glitter of countless stars. A warm wind blew over the Great Plains. They walked holding hands for a long while until the boy felt they were the only ones alive in a moonlit land.

The princess stopped and turned to him. "One day, we will find out who your real parents are." He looked up at the endless stars and sighed.

"I hope so. I want to know."

She cupped her hands around his cheeks and stepped closer. Her familiar scent of flowers enveloped him. He looked down at her face, bathed in the full moonlight. The dark, golden wheat fields spread out behind her. His breath caught at her incredible beauty. She looked up at him and leaned forward. Unbidden, he met her in the middle, and they kissed tenderly under the full moon surrounded by the endless Great Plains. When they finally parted, Chip exhaled in wonder. He was about to say something, but she put a finger to his lips and kissed him again. The boy realized there was no need for words. Afterwards, he did not remember how long they stood in the sea of gold under the stars, but it was perfect.

When they arrived back, holding hands and trying not to smile, Chase looked at them with narrowed eyes. They both gave an innocent shrug as if unsure of his expression. The tall boy grunted and then settled down on his cloak. Garth pulled out a tiny leftover portion of cheese and bread, which they devoured. None of them had much food left. Xander sat cross-legged, still muttering to himself, so the rest of them decided to go to sleep. They had no tents or pillows, so they spread their cloaks over the wheat, which provided a soft cushion that was quite comfortable. The wizard took the first watch, saying he was still mulling things over. The others did not argue.

The princess nestled close to Chip, who felt a deep connection of love and peace. The boy allowed the warm night breeze to lull him into a deep sleep.

The morning arrived with a colder wind. The companions had run out of food, and their water skins were almost empty. The wizard assured them they would not starve before reaching Banfar. The sun began to climb in the sky as they set out, and by lunchtime, the air warmed. The golden fields spread out before them endlessly until finally, by midafternoon, they could make out a black dot on the horizon. Their bellies began to growl, and they were completely out of water.

"I hope I'm not seeing things," Chase complained, squinting east.

"Fear not, my boy. That is indeed Banfar. Two hours at the most," Xander assured them. Chase grimaced, rubbing his stomach, and trudged on. He was in incredible shape but needed constant feeding. The boy had a large frame for his age and was almost as muscular as Garth. Going hungry tended to sour his mood.

They began to see the occasional farmer and helpers dotting the fields. The party passed close to some of the workers, who gave them a suspicious glance, which turned into indifference.

"Not the friendliest place," Chase noted.

"No. It will only get worse. Keep your wits about you," the wizard advised.

The black dot emerged into a huge town, if not quite a city. With the sun at their backs, they reached the main gates late in the afternoon. As they approached, two guards in stained uniforms appraised the party from the top of the gates. One was casually chewing on the end of a stalk of wheat.

The man disappeared, then opened the gates enough for him to saunter up to them, eyeing the princess up and down. Chip's face darkened.

"State your business," he slurred. The smell of alcohol and urine wafted off him.

"Picking up supplies and moving on, kind sir," the wizard said politely.

"Is she gonna stay and work?" he asked with a leer, jerking his thumb at Eleanor. The other guard also came through the gates, trying to get a better look. He gave a lecherous grin and nodded in approval. Before Chip could intervene, the weapons master moved in front of the princess to stand before the first guard. His face was a piece of chiselled granite.

"She travels with us," he said with a menacing tone. The man appraised Garth, eyes widening at the multitude of bristling weapons, then gulped.

"Can't blame you," the guard said, laughing. "I would keep her too. Carry on." He tried to slap the weapons master on the back as if they had shared a private joke, but Garth moved deftly. The man's hand met air, and he blinked in surprise. He was about to say something else, but the group had already moved on. Shrugging, the guard strolled back to the side of the gate and took a swig from a bottle on the ground.

"Well done," Xander said to his Protector. "Let's avoid a repeat of last time, shall we?" Garth grunted.

Eleanor noticed Chip's glower. She put a hand on his arm. "It's alright. I can handle myself. I am used to being gawked at by men and boys. This is a place where I expect it. Let us not draw attention to ourselves." She waited until Chip reluctantly nodded.

"I suggest we make our way to the Reindeer Inn," the wizard said. "It has the least offensive reputation. Unfortunately, we must go through the...seedier part of town to get there. It's called the Lower District."

They walked down the main thoroughfare, packed with all manner of folk. Hawkers lined the sides of the road, calling out their wares to anyone within sight. The shops were small and odd-looking, some with symbols on their signs. The noise was deafening. Groups of men stumbled down the street, obviously inebriated, shouting obscenities. Scantily clad prostitutes stood on corners or in front of alleys, trying to lure potential patrons. One drunken man tried to get in a free grab but received a swift high-heel kick between the legs. He flopped on the ground groaning while his friends pointed and laughed.

Guards walked by, most looking no better than the ones at the front gates. Some even strolled around with a drink, reeking of booze. Chase's mouth hung open in shock as his eyes went from one insane scene to the next. The smell of urine, alcohol, and incense filled the air. Chip noticed groups of people wearing dark cloaks standing motionless inside alleyways or store recesses, peering at the passersby. They were usually in front of shops with strange symbols on them.

"What are those stores?" he managed to ask Xander over the din.

The wizard followed his finger. "Those are the cults. Some of the symbols mean 'demon,' 'death,' or even 'murder.' The original meanings may have even been lost. The helmet and horns symbols are obvious, but the others with runes are anyone's guess. Some cults practice piety, while most believe satisfying human pleasures is the only purpose of life. They stand in front of their stores in judgment or to lure future members."

Even as the wizard answered, a man in a red cloak, hidden in a recessed storefront, stepped forward, barring their way. "The Demon King is coming," he hissed. Tattoos covered his face, and the skinny man's tongue was cleft in two. "We alone will be saved. Join us, for the time is now." He beckoned behind him to a store with the horned helmet on its awning. The doors were open, and inside they could make out others standing with long robes. As Chip started to look away, he noticed a blaze of green eyes and then felt a firm yank as Xander pulled him into the middle of the road to avoid the hissing man.

"Did the Dark Elf enter your mind?" the wizard whispered in Chip's ear.

"No."

"Good. I hope he did not recognize me." After several paces, they looked back to see a new figure in front of the store. This one wore a red cloak with a green fringe, staring after them from the cowl of his hood. His face was almost completely covered in shadow, but the boy thought he could make out almond-shaped black eyes. The man with the forked tongue, now in the middle of the road, was already beseeching other travellers to join his cause. "It seems the Dark Elves are already here," the wizard said grimly. The rest of the crowd converged behind them, and when they risked another glance back, the figure was gone.

It seemed that with every step they took, someone asked them to join a cult, buy some wares, or sell themselves. A large man strode up to Garth and opened his coat, showing a wicked row of curved daggers for sale. The weapons master shook his head, walked past, and then whirled around to grab the wrist of a skinny street urchin who was about to pick his pocket. The boy, no more than twelve summers old, hissed at him. "Find some honest work," Garth said and shoved the child into the large man, who he determined was his accomplice. After seeing Garth's expression, the man ushered the boy away, and they disappeared into the crowd. Xander nodded in approval.

"Hey there, cutie," a scantily clad woman in stained underclothes tried to reach for Chip. She had long, stringy hair and garish makeup that gave her a clownish look. "First time is for free." Her dirty fingernails extended to stroke Chip's cheek, but the princess slapped her hand away, scowling.

"He's mine already, honey," Eleanor growled, pushing between them. The prostitute huffed and then sidled up to Xander.

She rubbed herself grotesquely. "It's probably been a while, old man. Wanna feel young again?" She laughed raucously, tugging on the elbow of his cloak.

"I am quite flattered, young lady, but we have no money." The wizard pushed forward without waiting for an answer. She stopped, pouting, then turned around and looked for new business.

"Geez, I guess I'm chopped liver," Chase complained. "I was hoping for at least an offer." He tried to act serious but started laughing. Eleanor punched him in the arm. The crowds finally began to thin as they left the Lower District. Xander asked them to turn right at a smaller street, which looked darker and more sinister. He explained it was a shortcut to the more hospitable areas of town. Lone figures could be seen inside alleys or leaning against walls, smoking different types of pipes. Many faces were hollow with sunken cheeks. Some had emaciated bodies stuck in awkward, unnatural poses.

"Wack," explained Garth, seeing the puzzled expressions on the boys' faces. "It is a drug made from wheat and altered with dark magic. This place is a haven for new and deadly drugs. Many who start never get off and waste away to nothing."

"I thought we were trying to get to a nice part of town," Eleanor complained, looking at the dilapidated buildings and dark figures.

"As I said, it's a shortcut. It gets worse then better if memory serves." The wizard scratched his head. "Haven't been here for a while."

"You lost?" A rough-looking man with red hair slipped out from around a corner. He reached into his pocket, making them stop. Garth stepped forward calmly. "Or you looking for some Wack?"

"Passing through," said the weapons master. He began to move forward, but the man blocked him.

"No problem, but if you wanna walk through these streets, you pay the tax." His eyes were bloodshot. His unwashed body reeked of neglect. Garth started to walk forward again, and the man whistled sharply. Xander rolled his eyes. Within moments, nine other men came around the corner carrying various rudimentary weapons. "You picked a bad day to come through my part of town." The man moved back and pulled a long dagger from behind his back.

Xander stepped forward and looked at all ten men. "You are all about to die or be very injured in the next few moments. You are likely too stupid or strung out on drugs to listen to me, but as a courtesy, I am giving you the chance to walk away." The leader stared momentarily, then laughed with menace and tensed to lunge. "Wait, I will even pay you for your trouble. After all, you said if we pay the tax, we can go, right?"

The man paused, digesting the words in his addled state, then nodded. The wizard pulled two silver coins from his pouch. Unfortunately, clinking sounds could be heard, indicating he was retrieving the coins from a pile of others. The wizard grimaced, then tossed the two coins to the man who caught them with his free hand. "That should be more than ample. Let us pass." Xander smiled amicably.

The leader looked at each silver coin up close, then stepped aside, ushering the other nine back.

The companions walked forward, hands resting on their sword hilts. They got a dozen feet past the group when the man called out, "Actually, I changed my mind. This is not enough tax. I heard those other coins clinking. Double it, and you can pass." Chip noticed the weapons master's hand go white on his sword hilt.

Xander turned around. "No magic," he whispered to them. Chip nodded and guided the princess to the side. The wizard took two steps back, facing the men.

"I always have faith that humans will do the right thing. Everyone deserves a chance. You had yours. No matter what I give, you will continue asking for more. I will now offer you one last chance to let us be. It will be the greatest and last mistake you will ever make if you do not. In fact, if you do not listen, it will justify what we are about to do to you."

The thug reacted with surprise then looked at his nine burly friends. They all laughed heartily, except a slender fellow who assessed Garth and Chase then turned and ran. His purple coat flew horizontally in the wind as he bolted down the street and disappeared into another alley.

The leader scowled. "Pan is always scared of things. He only survives because he knows information. I tell ya, he's getting a good beating from me when I'm done here." The leader walked forward brazenly. The others followed, holding dangerous-looking cudgels and metal bars. Two carried hatchets.

As one, the companions pulled their swords. The men paused for a moment, then charged. They had no game plan or fighting experience. Chip, Chase, and Garth fanned out before the wizard and princess. The first three thugs tried to attack them with overhand strikes. The two boys blocked easily then disembowelled two of them. The weapons master did not even bother to block the strike of the third but stepped to the side and decapitated the man.

They methodically went through the other five men, blocking and parrying before finding openings and dispatching them. The leader stood in the back and began shaking. His eight companions were dead in moments. The man dropped his weapon and ran. Garth calmly pulled a throwing dagger from his belt and let it fly in one smooth motion. The knife buried itself to the hilt in the back of the man's neck, and he dropped to the ground unmoving.

Xander approached his body and pulled his two coins from the man's pocket. He heard the clink of other coins but did not touch them. Shaking his head, he rejoined the others.

"Some will never learn," he said ruefully.

"As you can see, it is hard to be discreet in Banfar," Garth commented. He looked at the boys, who cringed at the bodies, realizing these were not just demons they had killed but men. "It was you dying or them. Nothing we could have said or done would be enough. The wizard gave them their chance."

The weapons master cleaned his sword on a dead man's pant leg and stood up. Anyone else in the immediate area had skulked away as the fighting began. The boys both nodded and cleaned their weapons without comment.

"Let's go." Garth gestured for Xander to lead the way.

Chip turned at the last moment to look behind him and thought he saw a flash of purple disappear into an alley in the deepening gloom.

6

The party hurried down several smaller streets, occasionally needing to walk around a person stretched across the road. Twice, they found people lying in a pool of blood with throats slashed. Chip was shocked at the violence and lawlessness of such a city. It hurt him that humans, who had so much to live for, killed each other for no good reason.

Xander noticed his dismay. "Do not judge all men by the actions of a few. Addicts will sell their children to feed drug habits. This place is a cesspool of hopelessness and greed. Those men back there have committed unspeakable acts. Be merciful to them until it is obvious they spurn it, then be strong and do not hesitate. Evil exists in men, too, not only demons. Some even glorify it. Before this is over, you will see the depravity of humankind, but never forget the good."

He patted Chip on the back. The boy thought it over, knowing the wizard was right. He looked at the beautiful princess. As long as he had her, Chip thought, he would never forget the good.

They finally emerged onto a brighter street with houses in better repair. Two guards stood at one end wearing cleaner uniforms. They looked at them suspiciously for a moment, likely wondering if they were of the ruffian kind, then looked away, apparently satisfied. The companions continued, crossing two more streets before ending up on a large thoroughfare with supply stores and dining establishments. In the middle of the street sat the Reindeer Inn.

"Let's get rooms, then pick up supplies," suggested the wizard. Garth nodded, and they walked inside. The common room was full of tobacco smoke and servers bustling around tables full of men playing cards or eating stew. Chip noticed few children in the town besides street urchins and homeless kids. They were likely born here or abandoned, he thought sadly. Banfar was not the type of place to take a family. Pretty women in long dresses and makeup wandered the room, leaning down to whisper in men's ears.

Chase noticed it too, and they looked at each other, realizing what was happening. Xander led them to a long desk with several servers. Some people gave them curious glances, while others spied them more furtively. For the most part, they were ignored. Nobody seemed to want trouble at the Reindeer Inn.

"What can I get you?" a server asked while pouring several drinks.

"For now, rooms if you have any. We have money," Xander responded cordially.

"Money is good," she said with a grin. "Hang on." She looked through an open door at the back and yelled, "Quirk, they want rooms."

Xander grimaced. Half the common room looked over, studying them further.

"He will be with you in a moment." She skittered off, laden with full mugs. The wizard gave her a painstaking nod.

"So much for being discreet in Banfar," he said, echoing Garth's earlier statement.

"Real subtle," said Chase. Xander shot him a bushy glare. The tall boy gulped and hid behind the princess, which did not work well, given the size difference.

A small man with glasses arrived from the back room. "I'm Quirk. How many rooms, Mr?"

"Mr. Longfellow and two will suffice," the wizard said smoothly. "This is my son, nephews, and niece."

Quirk looked at the group curiously, but his eyes stayed on the princess for a moment too long. "Where did you come from, if you don't mind me asking? Families don't come here often."

"We come from a village east of Vanalon. Calgar is too full, so we decided to head up here to resupply. We are heading east to Toron," answered the wizard.

Quirk seemed to contemplate this then nodded. He leaned in, pushing his glasses higher up on his nose. His skin held an oily sheen. "Are the stories true? Did the demons attack Vanalon?"

Xander paused, deciding how to answer. "Yes, it's true. Vanalon fell but has since been retaken by Calgar. From my understanding, it still holds."

"Did you see the demons?" the man asked, leaning forward with bated breath, a strange look coming over his face.

Xander's eyes squinted slightly. "Yes. Not live ones, though. We saw some bodies on the side of the road. They were fearsome and evil. We decided to leave before meeting any."

Quirk's eyes widened, and he licked his lips. "Interesting." He feigned a laugh. "How many rooms?"

"As I said, two if possible."

"Oh, quite right. Two silver coins for each room."

Garth looked at the small man without changing expression. "That seems awfully expensive. This is not Toron."

Quirk shrugged. "Things are filling up. They are the only two left." He looked down for a moment. It was obvious he was lying.

Before Garth could respond, Xander slapped four silver coins on the table. "We will take them. I am hoping that the price includes a bowl of stew. We are quite hungry." Quirk was about to shake his head, but the weapons master gave him a look that would scare off a fanged black bear.

"Yes, that includes stew," the small man chirped, forcing a smile.

"And ale." Garth was not asking. The man nodded quickly.

Quirk reached under the counter and produced two keys. "Take the stairs on your left, then down the hall. The two rooms are at the end. Carry your stew with you. The tables are full."

There was clearly more than one empty table, but they did not cause a fuss. He went into the back and returned with a tray carrying five heaping bowls. He signalled to a server. "Carry these up with some drinks and show them to their rooms."

The woman nodded and poured out five large glasses of ale. She handed them out, grabbed the tray, and started up the stairs. The famished travellers followed her. Chase salivated as he eyed the steaming bowls. Chip noticed the small man watching them leave from the corner of his eyes.

The rooms turned out to be large and comfortable. Each had two cots with clean bedding, along with a couch, coffee table, desk, and chair. They decided to eat together in one of the rooms to talk. The server placed the large tray on the table and left to return with one extra cot she set along the wall at the back of the room. She excused herself, and everyone dug into their stew.

"What meat is in here?" Chase asked when he was halfway through.

"Prairie dog," said Garth shortly.

The tall boy's eyes widened, and he almost spat it out but shrugged instead. "I'm so hungry that if you said it had killer frogs, I would eat it." Chase wolfed down another heaping spoonful. "But not giant spiders. I'd pass on that one."

The weapons master grunted. "We need to get supplies before they close. We can cross the Great Plains and reach the Guild in two weeks with horses. There are lakes and ponds alongside the road where we can make camp. Sporadic villages also line the route where we can stable the horses and stay at an inn if they have one. We will leave in the morning. I figure we have, at most, two days before the destruction of Cave Mountain is discovered. A fast demon runner will then relay the message within three days back through the barrier. The Unnamed One will know we are no longer in Vanalon and have travelled east after destroying the mountain. With nothing to fear from us, the demon army may march on the city within a week."

Xander nodded grimly. "If the Demon King knows the wizard and red-eyed boy have left, he will initiate another attack on Vanalon with the help of his Inner Circle. What we did at the mountain was necessary, but it set the beginning of the Last Battle in motion."

They all looked at each other as the enormity of the statement set in.

"I'm still hungry," Chase said, holding out his empty bowl. This time, Xander slapped him in the arm.

"Don't you think of anything else, boy?" he shook his head and got to his feet. "Let us be off. Keep your wits about you. This part of town is better, but it is still Banfar." Chase rubbed his arm sheepishly.

They left the Reindeer Inn and turned down the busy street, breathing in the cool evening air. Food was still hawked at every corner, but the area was more civilized and much quieter. One proprietor sold roasted chicken with wheat noodles and corn. Chase tugged on the wizard's sleeve with baleful eyes until the old man gave in and ordered two whole chickens and sides.

They washed the crispy chunks down with another glass of ale. The princess was not used to the heady brew and seemed to find everything quite amusing afterwards. Street performers dotted the road at various intervals, some with large crowds throwing copper coins in a box and others with lesser skills trying to impress anybody that would look.

One performer was adept at juggling torches thrown high into the night sky. The group paused to watch if only to blend in. The princess found the act hilarious. Others in the crowd were trying to figure out why she was laughing so hard, which prompted Xander to signal to Garth that it was time to move on.

Chip grabbed her elbow and guided her away, which she somehow found even funnier. It was hard for him not to join in, as her laughter was infectious. He smiled, thanking the Creator again that she was in his life. As he directed her away, the boy caught a glimpse of a purple coat to his right, but when he looked fully, it was gone.

The weapons master continued navigating the crowds until they thinned out at the end of the street, where he stopped at a store with a row of horses tied out front. A large man with dark skin and heavily muscled arms walked out to greet the party.

"Mr. Stone and Mr. Wizard, nice to see you again. It's been a long time." He shook their hands with a meaty paw. "If I recall, last time I sold you horses, you were in quite a rush to head out west. Gosh, it must be going on more than fifteen years now."

"Quite right, Carl," Xander agreed. "I must admit we needed to get out in a hurry."

"You made it just in time. A short while after you left, the guards came up, led by the mage Scar. He did not look happy. When he asked if I sold you horses, I shrugged and said I did not recall ever seeing the two of you, as I have a really poor memory. Of course, seeing you now, I do recall selling you a lovely spotted brown stallion and a lively black mare. If I recall correctly, that is."

He smiled.

"Looks like your memory has improved," Xander laughed. "You are spot on."

"Great. I try not to forget a face or, for that matter, a business transaction. Where I do run into memory problems is when somebody else wants to get involved in someone else's business. I tend to get quite forgetful. So what can I help you with this evening?" The wizard looked at his Protector.

"We appreciate your discretion," Garth said respectfully. "We are looking for five horses to carry us to Toron." Chase was about to correct him on their destination but got a swift elbow from Chip.

"I see. It's a bit of a roundabout way of getting to Toron, but very well." Carl winked. "I bought the five at the end together so they get along with each other. Four stallions and a mare." Garth walked over, examining them with an expert eye, and nodded.

"How much?"

"Five gold coins with the saddles and bags," Carl said firmly.

"Fair," the weapons master said, glancing at Xander, who agreed. They shook on it. The wizard ruffled through his pouch while Carl saddled the horses. After the money exchanged hands, they all mounted. Eleanor took the white mare.

Carl stood to the side, muscular arms folded. "How bad is it out west?" he asked. "Is a demon army really coming as the fanatics rave?"

The weapons master looked at the horse trader. "Yes. Vanalon will likely fall in a week, Calgar a couple of weeks later. Cave Mountain will be crawling with them by month's end. I suggest you sell your remaining horses and seek safety in Toron."

Carl looked at him for a long moment then sighed. "It is as I feared, very well. May the Creator speed you in your travels." He reached up and shook the weapons master's hand then waved at the others.

They followed Garth back down the road to shop at other supply stores. The companions ensured that someone always waited outside with the horses while the others carried supplies. They purchased tents, spare clothes, sleeping bags, pots, soap, and other items until the saddlebags bulged. The last stop was at a food staple store near the flaming torch juggler.

"I will wait with the horses," Eleanor beamed. "I want to watch the juggler."

"I will stay too then," Chip offered, not wanting to leave her alone. He also enjoyed watching her laugh. The others went inside to buy food for the journey.

Chip breathed in the cool night air as he watched the princess, still sitting astride her horse, clapping as the juggler finished a trick. The flames from the torches flickered over her upturned face, and he had a sudden urge to kiss her.

At that moment, he saw a small hand snag a saddlebag off the back of her horse and then disappear. Eleanor noticed it too, looking indignant. The young thief ran past the princess, who leapt down to grab him but missed. It was the same street urchin who tried to pickpocket the weapons master.

"Get him," she shouted as he darted through the applauding crowd. No one noticed the thief, and even if they did, it was Banfar after all. Chip leapt off his horse and took off after the small boy who darted between people and horses, even carrying a full saddlebag.

The crowd began to thin, and he was able to catch up to the wily thief. Right before he grabbed the boy's collar, the urchin darted down an alley between two buildings.

Chip followed on his heels, squinting in the darkness. He did not see the punch coming from a man standing in the shadows, running straight into it. His mouth and nose erupted in a spray of blood, and a second punch to his stomach caused him to fall forward.

Chip groggily saw another man on the opposite side slash where his head had been with a long dagger. A wave of dizziness washed over him, and instinctually his training kicked in. Instead of landing on his face, he pushed with his feet and rolled in a somersault. It was a lucky move as the tip of a dagger only scratched between his shoulder blades instead of impaling him. Chip tried to regain his feet but was still too dizzy. Instead, he spun around to face his attackers, lying on his back. The boy with the saddlebag sauntered up to him, laughing.

The second man was yelling at the first. "What did you punch him for? I would have slit him ear to ear if you had let him be."

"I dunno. He was right in front of me. It hurt my hand, though," the first man grunted, shaking it.

Chip's mouth filled with the metallic taste of blood. His ears were ringing. The street urchin leaned down in front of him. "We are gonna get your friends too, rich kid. We already got the girl." He laughed and kicked him hard in the face, drawing fresh blood, then spat on him.

"Get out of the way, Spider," the second man said. "Let me skewer him."

Chip ignored his dizziness and the blood dripping off his face. He realized with shock that they had orchestrated the whole thing. Worse, the boy said they already had the princess. The second man walked up to him, holding his dagger out with a grin. He placed his feet on either side of his chest, lifting the blade high.

"This is going to hurt."

Chip's mind exploded with rage. His eyes blazed a ferocious red as he blasted through his Wall. The urchin leapt back in shock and bolted. The man brought the dagger down with full force, intent on burying it in the boy's chest. Before it could strike, Chip unleashed a torrent of red fire, blasting the man backwards and incinerating him from head to toe.

The first man who punched him was trying to run out of the alley, but the boy seized him with his Power, levitating him back to float before the enraged orphan. A urine stain appeared between the man's legs before Chip pulled every limb apart at the same time. Fountains of blood erupted in all directions, spraying his clothes and face. He did not care. He flung the man's torso aside and stood up, striding down the alley towards the street filled with Power. He burst onto the road, looking towards the horses. The princess was missing.

Someone yelled from the crowd, pointing at him. Blood covered him from head to foot as he stood there with red eyes blazing. If the people of Banfar ever believed that a monster had come to life, it was now. Most of the crowd screamed and ran. Some obvious cult members dropped to their knees, believing their salvation was at hand. The boy's other companions burst from the food store to see the commotion. Chase's jaw dropped at the sight of him, and even Garth's eyes widened. Xander assessed the situation quickly then looked around for the princess.

Chip walked up like a creature from the dead. "They've taken her," he managed through gritted teeth.

The wizard held up his hands in a calming gesture. "Do you require healing?"

"No, most of this blood is not mine."

"Tell us what happened?"

Chip quickly explained how the thief stole the saddlebag and lured him into the alley, where the two men ambushed him while others took the princess. "It was the same street kid who tried to pick-pocket you," he told Garth.

The weapons master nodded. "That gives us a place to start."

"His name is Spider."

"We must move fast," Garth said, turning towards the horses.

"The young thief will lead us to her. I suspect they are heading towards the Lower District. Mount up."

"Don't look now, but the guards are coming," Chase pointed.

A dozen men in stained uniforms were running towards them. The weapons master tied the white mare's reins to his saddle and leapt onto his horse. The others followed suit, and within moments they were galloping across the street as the guards arrived, screaming for them to halt.

They ignored the soldiers and raced towards the Lower District. Chip would not stop until he found the princess. His rage was like a bank of hot coals, spurring him forward. A sense of urgency filled him like never before. He could not lose her.

7

The weapons master led them down several alleys and across two more streets before turning into the Lower District, which brimmed with all types of people. Drunkards spilled out of taverns, staggering into other partygoers in the middle of the street. Hungry revellers ate cheap food in front of shouting street hawkers. On the sides stood dark forms wrapped in long cloaks, observing from the cowls of their hoods. Chip spied a small boy running with a group of men who carried something wrapped in a blanket before the crowd swallowed them up.

"There!" he yelled. Given the number of people on the street, they could not gallop, but Garth pushed through. They made it to the spot where Chip saw the group of men with the urchin. Ahead, the crowd became even thicker, replete with all manner of folk looking to satiate their needs. Prostitutes draped themselves over drunken men who puffed their chests out with male bravado while drug users wandered around wide-eyed, startled at every turn. In the background stood tall men in red or black cloaks looking for new membership.

Chip glanced at a dark alley to their left in time to see the man in the purple jacket standing behind a group of men with a smug look. Something about his calm expression gave the boy pause. He would not be caught off guard again.

The orphan instinctively wrapped himself in a red shield of Power and turned as a green ball of fire flew at him from a Dark Elf standing on the opposite side of the street. Not this time, he thought and held up his hand. A savage stream of red fire dissolved the ball and exploded into the Dark Elf's chest. He was dead before it exited his back. The boy turned to the group of men on his left who were already engaged with Chase and the weapons master. The man in the purple jacket now held a look of shock on his face and turned to run.

Chip reached out with a hand of Power and lifted him off his feet. The man windmilled frantically to no avail as the boy levitated him towards the street. An attacker struck Chip's arm with a heavy cudgel, but his red shield caused the wooden weapon to disintegrate. The thug had time to register a look of disbelief as he dropped the now-useless weapon before the orphan flicked his left hand in irritation. The man shot backwards into the stone corner of the alley, where his back broke with a loud snap.

The crowd shrieked, and people ran in all directions, not knowing where to go. A combination of reactions occurred, with some cloaked figures supplicating themselves while others screamed in horror, trying to escape. Some bystanders stood and watched the spectacle, enjoying whatever drug they were on.

Chip leapt off his horse and drew the struggling man with the purple coat towards him. The boy was covered in blood, and his blazing red eyes made the people shrink back in fear. The other attackers stumbled backwards to get out of his way. The crowd spread out, giving him a wide berth. He floated the man up to his bloody face.

"Where is she?" Chip's cracked lips oozed fresh blood, and his voice shook with raw Power.

The man looked at him in abject terror. "Are... are... you the One?" he asked in disbelief.

Chip did not expect such a question, but then it made sense. Some thought he was the Demon King come to life. "Yes. Now speak."

"Master, I am Pan," the man gasped, bowing his head. "We did not know it was you. Spider said you had red eyes, but we thought he was making it up. He lies all the time. Please forgive us."

"Where is she?" Chip repeated.

"We have taken the girl to the altar to sacrifice her for you."

Chip's face bristled with rage. "Where?" he screamed.

Pan pointed down the street. "In the basement ..." he stammered. "They are preparing her." The other attackers stopped, unsure of what to do. Most were already dead, lying in a heap in front of the alley. "Do not fight him! He is the One!"

They began falling on their knees, crying at the return of their beloved king. Chip ignored them and walked down the middle of the street, levitating the man with the purple jacket in front of him. What was left of the crowd parted as people scrambled over one another to get out of the red-eyed being's way. His companions followed close, holding their weapons at the ready.

"Show me where," Chip commanded. Pan pointed to the left. It was the same store they had seen on their arrival when the tattooed man with the forked tongue had tried to recruit them. The boy stopped in front and turned, facing the open door. The sign above the store showed a horned helmet.

"At the back, down the stairs," Pan directed. Chip walked in, startling figures on either side who stepped back in shock. "He's the One. It is our beloved king returned," the man with the purple jacket said to several people who lined the walls in long, blood-red cloaks. He started laughing with joy. "We are saved!"

The boy walked forward, eyes blazing. As one, the cloaked figures dropped to their knees and began to chant. A crowd started to gather outside the store. Rumours of the Demon King's return seemed to spread like wildfire.

Chip walked towards the back of the room to a heavy inset door covered with runes. He used his Power to tear it off its hinges and threw it to the side. The followers gasped and chanted even louder. Wide steps led downward to a flickering light. He floated Pan down the steps in front of him. The man's purple jacket hung straight down as he arched his back with glee.

The steps went deep into the ground. The walls became rough stone, and the boy realized this was an ancient place. The store was a front for an old cult that must have existed for centuries, even millennia.

Chip reached the bottom, which opened into a cavernous room. Dozens of cloaked figures dressed in red robes were packed on each side, totalling at least one hundred cult members. It was then that he saw her.

At the end of the room stood an altar of stone, and on the top rested her body. They had dressed Eleanor in a short white gown. Behind her stood a tall figure in a red cloak with a green fringe. The princess was not moving. Chip's rage was all-consuming.

"Behold, the Demon King!" the man in the purple jacket announced as he floated forward in ecstasy. The red figures dropped in supplication on both sides and began to chant. The sound reverberated off the stone walls in a rhythmic pounding that increased in crescendo.

The boy strode forward, covered in blood, eyes blazing.

"It's not him!" shouted a high-pitched voice near the altar. Chip noticed the street urchin stepping forward from a shadowed alcove at the back. "He tried to kill us."

"Spider is right," said a small man in a red cloak standing at the front. "It is her friends. He is just a boy." He pointed at Chip, turning to reveal his face in the torchlight. It was Quirk from the Reindeer Inn. Suddenly, the pieces fell into place. When they checked into the hotel, Chip noticed Quirk's prolonged stare at the princess. The inn clerk was a cult member who had singled her out for sacrifice to the Demon King. Now he understood. The boy's rage flared anew.

The tall, cloaked form behind the altar stepped forward.

"You are not my Master," the figure intoned, pulling back its hood to reveal the pale face of a Dark Elf with almond-shaped black eyes. Those eyes flared bright green as three figures to each side stood up and removed their hoods with eyes blazing. As one, seven Dark Elves shot green fire at him from both sides. Chip vaguely sensed Xander's magic come to life. The boy had already built up his Power, and now he could finally unleash his rage. As the green fire shot towards him, he covered himself with a thick red shield, absorbing it. Chip wanted to blast outwards and forwards, incinerating everything in his path, but he did not want to risk striking the princess.

Instead, he threw the man with the purple coat, still with a dreamy smile, directly at the Dark Elf behind the altar with deadly force. The sound of their bones breaking on impact briefly exceeded the noise of the members' incessant chanting. Next, he lifted the three Dark Elves on either side of the altar and repeatedly slammed them into each other. Black blood sprayed over the entire room, covering red robes with dark spots. Other cult members began screaming in terror, unsure what to do. Several launched themselves, trying to pull him down. Their hands melted as they touched his Power, and their robes caught fire.

"Kill the girl!" shouted Spider, running towards the princess, knife drawn to plunge into her chest. At the same time, Quirk screamed and ran at Eleanor with a wicked curved dagger. Chip could not bring himself to hurt a child, even one as evil as Spider, so he wrapped the princess in a red shield instead.

The urchin leapt anyway, his small face a mask of hate, and plunged the knife into her chest as he landed on top of her. The blade, his small hand, and finally, Spider's body melted as the young thief let out one last shriek. Quirk's knife and hand incinerated as he tried to slash her throat. He looked at the bloody stump of his arm, then turned and ran savagely at Chip, trying to claw his face with his remaining fingers. He rebounded off the boy instead, and his robe caught fire. The inn clerk ran screaming into the back wall, knocking himself out before succumbing to the flames. Chip's rage lessened as sadness filled him. He could not believe people, especially children, could be corrupted to such a degree.

The orphan looked around him, watching the red-cloaked members milling about in shock. Some were running into walls on fire, others threw themselves at him and melted, while several were still prostrate chanting their dark hymn.

Chase and Garth cut down any who tried to attack. The boy shook his head and walked to the front of the room, putting his hand on the motionless princess. The red shield surrounded them both. He reached into her mind and body and felt a sluggishness, indicating she had been drugged. Otherwise, she seemed unhurt.

With his magic, he dissolved the substance flowing through her veins, then removed the blood on his face and clothes. He healed his face and gently urged her to wake. He watched as her eyes opened, and she looked up at him.

"What happened?"

"You are safe." With both wrapped in a single cocoon of red Power, the boy leaned down, kissed the princess, and pulled her up to a sitting position. She looked around the cavernous room and gasped. Bodies littered the ground, and blood covered everything. The remaining figures in red cloaks huddled in terror against the wall, guarded by the weapons master and Chase, who held their swords at the ready. Xander stood behind them with blue eyes blazing.

"Good grief. What happened here?" the princess gasped.

"Well, without sugar coating it, the cult members were about to sacrifice you to the Demon King, who they thought was me," Chip said. She looked at him in horror. "I will explain later."

"Oh dear."

He turned and stepped forward in front of the altar. His red eyes blazed bright, but now the blood was gone from his face and clothes. He looked like a fearsome young wizard come into his Power.

"Show your faces," he commanded. "Now!"

The remaining figures in red cloaks pulled their hoods back. He was surprised to see some young faces, a few of them female. Most had fearful, sheepish looks on their faces. Others were prostrate in supplication, too scared to look up.

"Rise."

They slowly stood up and revealed themselves but one refused. Chip pulled the recalcitrant figure's hood back with his Power. It was the man with the tattooed face and forked tongue who accosted them when they entered the city. His lips curled back in a snarl.

"You are not the Demon King!" the man hissed.

Chip stepped forward. "No, I am not. I am the one who will kill him." He looked around with an aura of Power. "The Demon King's disciples, the Dark Elves, have recruited and brainwashed you. They control the demons who will run through this city and kill you without thought. The king you worship is really an ancient Dark Elf Prince who hates humans. He does not want to save you. He wants to destroy the human race. You have been lied to and offered a salvation that will never come. This is your opportunity to stop hiding behind your hoods and fight the demons. Only if all humans unite do we stand a chance."

The tattooed man spit on the ground. "I only serve my Master, the true Demon King!" There was a blur of motion as Garth sliced his head off with one clean sweep. It rolled across the ground, stopping face up. The forked tongue hung out of the man's dead face, forever frozen in a rictus of hate.

"You have been warned," the weapons master intoned in a menacing voice. "Anyone breaking the laws of the High King of Dominor by assisting the demons will receive the same fate. You all have a chance you do not deserve. I suggest you heed the...Guardian's advice. He is the Guardian of Humanity and our only hope." The weapons master turned to Chip and bent a knee. The boy's eyes widened, and he tried to shake his head, but the red-cloaked members followed suit. Xander nodded with a look of realization.

"All hail the Guardian of Humanity," the wizard intoned, bowing low. Chase looked confused, then shrugged and did the same. The princess stood beside Chip, curtsied, and held his hand. The boy was dumbfounded, looking at an entire room full of people bowing to him.

Eleanor tugged his elbow. "Let's go," she whispered. "You have to time things for full effect. I will teach you." She pulled him by the hand, and they walked out and up the stairs. He maintained the shield, having no idea what to expect outside. The others rose and followed. They exited the store and entered the street to find themselves in the middle of a large, milling crowd of people and guards.

Seeing his terrifying red eyes, everyone pressed backwards, giving them a wide berth. Two figures hidden in black cloaks did not. Chip saw a flash of green on either side of him, and he instinctively strengthened his red shield, surrounding them both. Roiling ropes of green magic struck him and the princess simultaneously. The crowd gasped in shock, and several people screamed.

The shield held easily as he lifted a hand to fling a Dark Elf with hurricane force into the top of a stone building on the other side of the street. The body erupted in a fountain of black blood. With his left hand, he released a flow of red magic into the other Dark Elf, who caught fire and crumpled, disappearing into a smoking pile. Some people passed out in the crowd, while others shouted in amazement. Chip's companions came out behind him, followed by the ones in red cloaks. Xander maintained his hold on the Power, eyes blazing bright blue.

"What is the meaning of this?" a loud, deep voice boomed. Everyone looked for the source. A group of guards stood at one end of the crowd, which had pushed back a good thirty feet, forming a large circle. "Get out of my way!" They still could not see who was talking. There was a bustle of movement among the guards, and finally, a dwarf pushed through to stand in front of them.

"Ah, Scar. To what do we owe the pleasure?" asked Xander, trying to hide his amusement. It was hard to see in the flickering torchlight, but the dwarf did indeed have a long scar running from his ear to the corner of his lip. His reddish hair stuck out in several directions, and his eyes had a mad look. The small man wore a black tunic and miniature brown pants.

"You know damn well, wizard," the dwarf growled. He looked at Chip's blazing eyes, and some bravado seemed to leave his face. Scar glanced back to ensure his guards were nearby and asked, "Who are you?"

"He does not answer to you," Xander said, stepping forward. The old man cleared his throat, then announced in a voice all could hear. "Ladies and gentlemen, before you stands the Red-Eyed Wizard, the Killer of General Morgo, the Bane of the Inner Circle, the Exterminator of Dark Elves, the Life Ender of Demons, the Jailer of the Dim, the Destroyer of Cave Mountain, the Black Dragon Slayer, and above all the Guardian of Humankind."

He stepped aside with a flourish, pointing at Chip.

There was a moment of complete silence. It was likely the first time in the city of Banfar's history that the Lower District was dead quiet. Chip stood in the middle of the street, staring at the wizard in shock, then looked at the crowd. Even the dwarf waited on him.

He finally took a step forward. Although it was not his thing, Chip decided to use the platform to save as many lives as possible. He would play the part if it meant helping even a single person.

"The wizard speaks true," he said, raising his voice. There were several intakes of breath. "We come from the besieged city of Vanalon, having fought a sizable demon army that broke through the barrier and attacked us over a week ago. In the end, they were defeated. We killed their general, many Dark Elves, and the demons themselves. I also killed the Demon King's black dragon, Fang."

More gasps erupted from the crowd. The dwarf's face changed from anger to disbelief.

"The demons are controlled by Dark Elves whose black eyes switch to another colour when wielding magic. In turn, the ones who control these Dark Elves are called the Inner Circle. The Demon King, an ancient Dark Elf Prince who practices black arts, commands them all. His thirst for power led him to kill his father, Elf King Galal, and cause the Breaking four millennia ago. We were able to contain him after the Great Battle a thousand years later, but now the barrier weakens.

"You are sadly mistaken if you think the Demon King will spare your lives. He has no honour, goodness, or sense of right from wrong. He is pure evil. His demons will run through the countryside and feed off every living thing. They come in all manner of shapes and sizes. They hunger for human flesh and thirst for your blood. Any promises made to you by those Dark Elves are empty. You will not be saved. At best, you will be slaves and slowly fed to his demon pets. At worst, you will be tortured for his amusement and then fed to them anyway."

He saw an older teenager with a tattoo of a horned helmet on his forehead at the front of the crowd, surrounded by a group of street kids. A skinny, taller boy with blond hair stood behind him, whispering in his ear, but he could not see his face. A pang of sadness went through him.

"Today, I watched a boy named Spider leap to his death on the conviction that we are somehow the evil ones, and the Demon King is the saviour. He died for no reason, and so will you if you listen to the false promises of these cults. I suspect many of you have ended up in Banfar because society rejected you. I would know because I was an orphan left at the gates of Vanalon as a baby. I understand how you feel."

Some in the crowd nodded and wiped at their eyes, holding hands.

"The end is coming. The demons will be attacking the human cities within the month. You will not be able to stop them. Gather your things and make for Toron. The human race will make a stand there. It may seem your life has no purpose anymore. You may feel you have done unforgivable things. You may have failed in everything you have ever tried to do. I am here to say that you have another chance. Leave the life of crime and drugs behind. Treat everyone around you with respect and love one another. Go to Toron and enlist. Your life can have a purpose. You can have hope. I will be there to challenge the Demon King in the Last Battle. I hope you will fight with me."

There was complete silence. Chip turned to see the back of the skinny blond boy as he walked away. He looked down sadly, realizing his message did not get through.

Then, the young man with the forehead tattoo began to clap, and cheers erupted in the crowd as people started to chant, "All hail the Guardian!"

The dwarf stepped forward, raising his hands. The crowd slowly quieted.

"These claims are unverified. The red eyes could be a simple parlour trick. I will conduct an investigation into the matter. As the Keeper of the City of Banfar, I must uphold the law." He pointed his finger at the wizard and the weapons master. "You, Xandrostika, and you, Garth Stone, are charged with the murder of nine men earlier today not two blocks from here. We have witnesses. In addition, three men were killed in a bar fight sixteen years ago when you passed through on your way to Vanalon. You will answer for those crimes too."

Xander held up his hands apologetically. "Please, Mr. Keeper, do not forget the fifty-odd cult members we just killed in the basement of this store." The dwarf's eyes widened. He was about to speak, but the wizard continued in a louder, more serious tone. "I, Grand Wizard Xandrostika, second only to High Wizard Balor, on behalf of the Wizard's Guild, and as a designated advisor to High King Dominor of Toron, charge you, Scar, with treason against Amrika. You have allowed these cults to flourish unchecked for far too long. You have allowed thievery, murder, and illegal drug use to thrive while you pad your pockets. Former Wizard Scar, I strip you of your title as Keeper, strip you of your membership in the Wizard's Guild, and banish you from Banfar."

This time, the silence was longer. The dwarf's face contorted, but no sound came out. The scar along his cheek wriggled like a snake as he tried to settle on an expression. "How dare you?" he finally managed. "Guards, seize them!" With that, the dwarf's eyes blazed blue, and he shot a fireball straight at Xander. The wizard quickly formed a circular blue shield and absorbed the impact.

Garth and Chase drew their weapons, looking like chiselled

warriors. The guards, most with stained shirts and bleary-eyed from drinking, weakly drew their swords but did not advance. The sight of the weapons master bristling with implements of death would make anyone pause.

Xander stepped forward, raising his hands. "My turn," he said in a voice filled with Power. The dwarf suddenly shot into the air and hung suspended in the middle of the crowd. He shrieked in terror and weakly shot another fireball, which Xander swiped away. The wizard turned his hand, and the dwarf flipped upside down. The blood rushed to the little man's face as he started waving his arms comically.

"Help!" he screamed.

The crowd started to snicker. The guards looked around uncertainly, and some began to chuckle. The wizard twirled his fingers, and the dwarf started spinning faster and faster. His cries became higher pitched until they sounded like a small child whining. The crowd laughed uproariously, and the guards lowered their weapons, enjoying the spectacle. Many had satisfied smiles on their faces. It was obvious the soldiers did not like their diminutive leader.

"Fetch me a horse," the wizard commanded one of the guards. The man hesitated. "I am, as advisor to High King Dominor, the senior representative here, and you will obey the chain of command. Fetch me a horse." The guard paused a moment longer, then saluted and waved to the other soldiers, who pulled a mount from the fringe of the crowd to the front. Xander plopped the dizzy dwarf onto the saddle with a loud thump. Scar's face contorted in confusion, and he started sliding off. The wizard used his Power to tie the reins around his short body, holding him in place. With that, he gave the horse a loud slap on its rump, and the crowd parted as the beast galloped towards the gates of Banfar. Loud cheers erupted from everyone, including the soldiers.

"Who is second in command?" Xander asked when the cheers quieted.

"I am, sir. Captain Morris here." A middle-aged guard pushed forward with a clean shirt.

"Send guards to ensure he does not return," the wizard instructed. "If the dwarf tries, warn him that he will be executed if he sets foot back in the city. From here on out, I want your men to abstain from drinking while on duty. They will wear clean shirts at all times."

He looked around at the storefronts and raised his voice.

"Henceforth, any cults of demon worship or dark arts are banned. No store can have a symbol on its sign. Anyone caught will be jailed, banished, or executed as the courts see fit. Punishments for thievery and murder will be strictly enforced. Illegal drugs, such as Wack, must be eradicated. Those caught dealing it will be severely punished."

He looked at the crowd.

"For those wishing to enlist in the upcoming war, line up at the administrative building in the morning. You will be given rations and escorted to Calgar or Toron. Food and lodging will be provided while you train. For others who cannot fight, you need to think of an orderly evacuation."

He turned back to the captain.

"My Protector, who also happens to be the High Commander of Vanalon, will advise you on the city's defence for those who remain. You are two days from Cave Mountain, so your assistance with scouting reports will be vital to the war effort. The grain surrounding us is also a food staple that needs to be harvested and sent on secure supply routes to feed the armies. If we survive this war, Banfar can become prosperous.

"Many jobs will need filling to achieve these goals. There is an ample supply of citizens here that need work. We will discuss this more in the morning. For tonight, have the guards dispose of the bodies in the basement of this store. Tomorrow, we will search the city for more Dark Elves or cults that persist. Finally, four stallions and a white mare should be nearby, assuming no one has tried to steal them. Find the horses and bring them here."

Captain Morris saluted. "Right away, sir." He turned and issued orders.

Xander looked at Garth. "We have much work to do and very little time. I had hoped to pass through here, but we cannot overlook Banfar's strategic advantage. The supply routes must be protected. I am surprised Dominor has not sent an emissary here to coordinate things. He may feel this city is a lost cause, but the High King is mistaken. The Unnamed One will unlikely attack Banfar anytime soon, as his focus will lie on Calgar and Toron. This city is the closest one we have to Cave Mountain. That is where the scouts come in. They can keep tabs on demon activity."

Garth agreed. "I will see to the city's defences in the morning and advise them on a proper retreat plan. How long do we have?"

The wizard made some quick mental calculations. "I am expecting demon trackers to reach Cave Mountain by tomorrow. Once they send their message back to the Demon King, he will know we are not in Vanalon anymore and siege the city. We can stay here two days more, but no longer. It is not a lot of time, but you can set a proper chain of command and put plans in place."

The weapons master nodded.

Several people from the crowd came forward to thank them for saving the city and giving them a chance. The older boy with the helmet tattoo approached Chip awkwardly and murmured his thanks.

"What is your name?" Chip asked.

"They call me Rabbit," he said quickly, looking down.

"How old are you?"

"Seventeen summers, I think."

Chip reached up and dissolved the tattoo with his Power. The brown-haired boy rubbed his forehead in wonder.

"Thanks. I'm an orphan too."

"Come tomorrow then," Chip said. "Line up at the administrative building, and they will give you a job, clothes, and food."

"You don't understand. I've done bad things," Rabbit said, grimacing.

"All the more reason to do good things," Chip said. "Listen to me. Not even the Creator himself can change what happened in the past. Let it go. You would not have come up to me if no good was left in you. Today is a new day and you have a chance to right all your wrongs.

"Do not get caught up blaming anyone or anything for what happened to you in the past. If you do, it will take the responsibility off yourself, allowing more bad decisions that you will blame on others. Take ownership of every choice you make from now on. Look at the bad things that happened to you as a chance to grow. Look at adversity and suffering as a challenge, and you will become stronger by that simple realization. Remember, it is the pressure that forms a diamond.

"So when bad things happen to you, smile. Today is a new day, and you have more information than you did yesterday. No more excuses, Rabbit. I will find you at the Last Battle and see what you have made of yourself."

The boy raised his chin and looked at Chip with wet eyes.

"Who taught you to be like this?" Rabbit finally managed, lip trembling.

Chip laughed and pointed at Garth. "He did," Xander grunted. "Oh, and him too." He pointed at the wizard and laughed again.

The weapons master turned to Rabbit and gave him a hunk of bread and cheese from his saddlebag. "Eat this tonight and report to the administrative building at dawn." The boy nodded, taking the food gratefully.

"I won't disappoint you." Rabbit gave them one more look of wonder, then disappeared into the crowd.

"Think he will come?" asked Xander, looking at his Protector.

Garth paused. "After the speech the Guardian made, how could he not?" He looked at Chip, smiled, and then arched an eyebrow. "It's the pressure that forms a diamond. I never taught you that."

Chip laughed. "No, you didn't, but it makes sense. What kind of pupil would I be if I couldn't come up with a few of my own?"

Garth patted him on the shoulder. "I have to admit that is a good one."

Others came, and the boy offered similar advice. Soon after, the guards arrived with their horses. Captain Morris saluted. "They were in an alley up the street rooting through garbage. I expected someone to steal them but the commotion here was such that even the thieves stopped to watch." He grinned. "I also wanted to say that I am happy Scar is gone. He required me to do things I'm not proud of and welcome the chance to make amends."

Garth stepped forward. "That's good to hear, Captain. It is never too late to change. We have much to do. I will see you at dawn in front of the administrative building." They both saluted.

8

The companions mounted their horses and departed the Lower District. By this time, the crowd had swelled as word spread of the battle between the Guardian and the cult. Cheers erupted, and shouts of thanks rang out as they left. A large group followed them on the off chance something else might happen.

Chip released his hold of the magic and swayed momentarily on his horse but still felt strong. He was growing in the Power. This was the longest he had maintained a hold on it, and he felt a strong pang of regret in letting go. The Power was like a thrilling elixir to him, probably not so different from the drug Wack. The thought disturbed him.

The boy knew that creating a bad habit was the fastest way to get addicted to something. The weapons master had told him, "The mind never forgets a habit, so make it a good one." A person's bad habits should be replaced as soon as possible, but the old habits will always be there. The brain keeps them all, good and bad. It is the human condition. Eventually, the good habits will replace the bad ones and lessen their strength. He knew it took willpower to get to the point where the new habit overpowered the old. The orphan felt his Power should be used as a last resort lest he start to rely on it. The

Demon King and Dark Elves were perfect examples of what could happen if someone habitually used their Power.

Chip accepted life's aches, pains, and weariness now that he had released his magic. He focused on taking in the good parts of Banfar. As terrible as some people were in this city, there was still much good. Almost everybody deserved a second chance. He felt a deep sadness for the young boy Spider. If Quirk had not tried to attack the princess at the same time, he would have been able to restrain the child. Things regrettably did not work out that way, for he had to protect the princess first. Chip would take the advice he gave the street kid Rabbit and not dwell on the past. Many humans would die before this war was over. He would do the best he could, knowing he could not save everyone.

They reached the Reindeer Inn and gave the reins to the stable man. Garth took out some food and other supplies they needed for the evening. Xander flipped the man a silver coin. "Keep a good eye on them and our supplies."

The groom nodded, looking at the coin in wonder. They walked through the common room, receiving many stares and fearful looks, which meant some patrons had already heard the tales. Xander walked up to the large desk at the back. The inn manager looked at him apprehensively.

"Can I help you, sir?" his voice quavered.

"Yes. I wanted to let you know that Quirk will not be showing up for work." He smiled and walked away.

"Oh, very well, sir. Do you know when he will be coming back?"

"Yes," Xander said without turning, "Never." The manager looked at him with raised eyes then shrugged and returned to his paperwork.

They reached the wizard's room to discuss the day's events before retiring. "It has been a long day and night," Xander said. "Until we get to the Guild, we must be careful. The Dark Elves have been here for a few weeks, perhaps longer. Many are spies sent by the Unnamed One to gather information and corrupt those in power. For now, they seek followers, but only to weaken the cities for easier pillage. Today, we saw something emerge, even in the darkest of places. That something is hope. We must hold on to it tight, for a great darkness is coming. May the Creator protect us."

The weapons master nodded. "I have no problem receiving blessings from the Creator. However, strategy and planning win wars, not blessings. From my experience, the most we can hope for is a little luck while we prepare for the worst. That is all I ask."

"You gave a good speech today, young Guardian." Xander smiled.

"Really?" Chase interjected. "The bane, the exterminator, the jailer? Wow."

"I think it was poetic," Eleanor chimed in, "and true."

"I do not like public speaking," Chip apologized to everyone. "I did the best I could."

"It was actually pretty darn good," Chase admitted.

"That is because you spoke from the heart," the wizard said warmly. "Who knew you could be such a motivator?"

"Must have had a good teacher," Garth added.

The wizard glanced at him sourly. "It takes a village, my friend."

The weapons master grunted, "Indeed."

Chip looked at Xander. "How did the dwarf Scar get his, well, scar?"

"Oh, that," the wizard scoffed. "I gave it to him."

The boy patiently waited for more. Xander smoothed out his robe. "How?" Chip finally asked, taking the bait.

"Oh, it is a burn mark. We had a little duel over a young woman in the Guild. He did not do so well. My punishment was to clean out the latrines for a week." The old man shuddered.

"Why didn't you heal him?"

"Dwarves do not like to be healed. They wear their scars with pride, even when they lose."

"Why did he say you killed three men on your way to Vanalon?" Chip asked.

The wizard glanced at Garth, who looked down and adjusted his weapons. "Well, that was another little misunderstanding. A group of men thought they could rob an old man who was urinating in an alley outside a certain bar. They did not see he had a Protector."

The boys' eyes widened at the weapons master, who shrugged.

"I see." Chip could not help but grin. "I'm just happy we are all together again." He glanced at the princess.

"You three are sleeping in the room next door with the extra cot," the wizard instructed, giving Chip an unreadable look. The boy nodded, trying not to look at Eleanor, who squeezed his hand even tighter. Chase rolled his eyes. "Alright. It has been a long night. Off to bed with you. Keep your doors locked. We old men need our sleep." Garth arched an eyebrow but did not respond.

They bid each other goodnight. The three entered the adjoining room and prepared their cots. Chip ensured the door was locked and pulled the desk over to block it for extra measure.

"Thanks, Mr. Guardian." Chase bowed low.

Chip tried to punch him in the shoulder, but he dodged it. "The name wasn't my idea," he laughed.

"It did sound pretty cool. I have to say you did do all those things." Chase flopped onto his cot, and his voice turned sober. "We killed people today. It was different from the demons. It was more personal and…. sad. The demons are bred to kill, but humans do not have to. It is such a waste." He shook his head.

"I know. I am still wrapping my head around it." Chip sat on his cot. "We have both trained for a long time, but taking a life is different. We had these notions growing up of grand adventures and killing the bad guys. I never thought it would be like this. The blood, the pain, the sadness. Now that we are doing it, it is not what I expected. I prefer the adventure part."

Chase nodded, serious for once.

"The higher the privilege, the higher the duty," the princess intoned. The boys gave her a puzzled look. "When someone is wealthy or has power, they should, out of duty, make responsible decisions for the good of others. Otherwise, they are selfish, greedy, or simply uncaring. As a princess, my mother taught me these things. Barton and Rupert did not handle their duties well. You two both have special qualities and talents that come with an accompanying duty. It is your test in this life. At least that is what my mom used to say." Her eyes grew distant. "I pray the Creator keeps her safe," she murmured. The princess looked at them with wet eyes. "We do not fight only for us. Our positions are such that we bear a greater responsibility. We fight for all humanity. In a way, we are all guardians."

The boys looked at her, and for a moment, all three felt like small children again. The princess, the orphan, and the squire's son, put together by fate or chance, they knew not. Looking at each other, they smiled.

"All for one," Chase said, grinning.

"And one for all," Chip finished.

"Except when I am undressing," the princess admonished. "Now turn away." They did as told while she undressed and slid under her blankets. "Now let us count sheep to see who sleeps first."

Chase blew out the candle on the desk. "One," the princess said with a giggle. The last thing Chip remembered was Chase mumbling a number that sounded like eleven.

They awoke mid-morning feeling a little guilty for sleeping in but refreshed. Under their door was a note from Xander, telling them to grab breakfast in town and meet them at the administrative building when finished.

Three silver coins were on the paper. They each took one. Chip's eyes widened at holding that much money. He had never had any. Eleanor gave him an amused look but said nothing. They washed and dressed, turning away at the princess's behest at appropriate times until they were clothed and ready to go.

When the trio reached the common room, it was abuzz with the previous night's events. Several patrons noticed them and elbowed their friends. Within moments, the entire room was silent.

"Awkward," Chase remarked, crossing the common area towards the front entrance. Chip and Eleanor followed.

A voice called out from the back, "Hail the Guardian." Several others echoed the cry. Chip smiled with embarrassment and nodded.

They exited the Reindeer Inn and blinked in the late morning sun. A large crowd had gathered outside, cheering and applauding. They had likely waited all morning to catch a glimpse of him. The princess laughed, and Chase expressed disbelief.

It was the peculiar crackle of magic that alerted Chip, and he instinctively knew something was wrong. His expression turned from a sheepish one to instant alertness. The boy saw a rope of green fire lash out at him from the corner of his eye. The Wall appeared in his mind, but he knew it was too late.

Making an unconscious decision based on his training, Chip launched himself into his friends, knocking them off their feet. The fire seared the side of his body, setting his shirt on fire and burning his exposed skin. He screamed in pain, then smashed through his Wall. Even as he did, more green fire struck him from the other side as he tried to rise. It hit him in the chest and face, knocking him backwards and melting his clothes. He experienced a searing pain across his lips, and his eyelids felt like they had burned away.

In agony, the boy pulled in his Power, wrapping his body in a red cocoon. Healing himself was not as simple as removing blood from his face, though he was able to extinguish the fire. He reached out with his presence and found the princess.

"Help, heal me!" he sent to her, writhing in pain. Chip sensed her to his left, maintaining a brown shield of Power. He pushed up one seared eyelid to see more Dark Elves appear and a blurry image of Chase trying to run at them with a sword. A fireball hit his best friend's shoulder, sending him cartwheeling off to the side. The elves began breaking through Eleanor's shield with their combined might. Chip could not see well, so he wrapped red magic around all of them.

The princess then directed her Power to heal him, removing the heat from his face and chest and restoring his skin. She cried out in agony at absorbing such severe injuries, which pushed his rage to new limits. He did not allow her to repair the burns on his arm but instead used the pain to fuel his anger.

The boy opened his eyes, seeing clearly. Before him, in different areas of the crowd, a dozen Dark Elves were pointing at them, all unleashing jagged lines of fire. Two of them were at the Brown Level, and he felt the strength difference in their magic. His shield held, and he paused to let his rage mount.

Most of the crowd had dispersed to stay out of the lines of fire, which gave him a clear view of all the magic wielders. Some were already running out of Power. Eleanor whimpered off to the side.

Chip could not contain his rage any longer. The boy raised his burnt arm and settled his gaze on the strongest Brown Level. "Burn," he said through clenched teeth, and a ball of red fire exploded with lightning speed at the Dark Elf, who blew apart in a shower of flesh and blood. He did the same to the next half dozen, one after another. Their dying screams were like a morbid symphony of death and destruction. He was the conductor.

For the final five Dark Elves, Chip lifted them into the air at the same time, filling them with red Power. They popped like cherries, drenching the street with black blood. Then, there were none left. A dead silence settled over everything. He saw Chase squirming on the ground and immediately reached out to heal his burns. His tall friend stopped writhing and sat up with an angry expression. Chip turned to the princess with a look of concern. She was trying to rise.

"Are you alright?" he asked, taking her hands.

"Yes, how did you hold in such pain? I would have healed you faster, but they were focused on my shield. Two of them were Browns." She got up slowly, showing signs of weariness, but stood straight. She looked him over and gasped, "Your arm!"

"It's alright," he said, brushing it aside. "You've done enough for now."

Chase ran up to them, teeth clenched. "I should have seen them in the crowd. It's my fault."

"We all should have been more vigilant," the princess concurred.

"No, it's my job. I am at fault. Responsibilities, remember?" Chase said, shaking his head.

"I did not mean it that way," Eleanor corrected. "You are not our Protector."

"Actually, I am."

"Says who?"

"Um, Garth." Chase looked down. "It's been my job for a long time now."

"Really?" Eleanor mused. "Well, then it is your fault." She laughed and poked him in the ribs. Chase glowered, trying not to smile.

Now that the danger was over, the crowd started moving back. Chip still clutched the Power, refusing to be caught off guard again.

"Well, there's one good thing," Chase said, his face lightening. "At least we probably killed all the Dark Elves left in Banfar. That was easier than rooting them out."

Chip thought about it and had to agree. "Let me try something." He sent his Power out like a blanket over the crowd, seeing if he could sense any other magic wielders. Of course, he knew they would have to be using magic for him to sense anything.

Dark Elves had a constant connection with their Wall down, but the connection was too faint unless they drew in and used their Power. Only Morgo had the unique skill of sensing another's Power from a distance, even if they were not using it.

Chip was about to give up and then felt something by the gates at the end of the city. A strong pulse of magic occurred. By the feel of it, he knew it was a Dark Elf. It looked like there was at least one left, after all. He surmised that this one was likely using magic to escape through the gates and report to his Master.

A contingent of guards appeared from a side street on horseback. They rode up to them, saluting. "Captain Melvin here. Wizard Xander sent us regarding a disturbance… Do you need…" He looked around at the scene of destruction and gulped. "Never mind, it looks like you have taken care of everything yourself, Mr. Guardian. Do you require an escort to the administrative building?"

Chip noticed the crowd seemed more enamoured with him. Screams of "All Hail the Guardian!" rang out, and he could hear other scattered shouts.

"You should have seen how he made them explode."

"His fire burned a hole right through them."

"The Dark Elves almost got him."

"He will save us all!"

More people were gathering by the moment.

"Yes, please escort us," he accepted as the shouts grew louder.

The captain saluted. "Men, form up."

The companions mounted their horses, which had just come from the stable. The guards formed a phalanx around them and escorted the group through the large crowd to a less congested cross street. With an open road in front, Captain Melvin urged the horses into a trot, leaving the crowd in the distance.

After a series of left and right turns through streets and alleys, they burst onto a park, which led to a large administrative building. A long line of citizens stretched across the green grass from the building to the main road.

As they rode by, shouts sounded up and down the line, cheering the Guardian. Chip was not sure what to make of it. They reached the front of the line, where Captain Morris sat at a long table with several others, processing people who wanted to enlist. Captain Melvin leaned down to apprise Morris of the situation.

Xander hurried over, taking in the boy's arm. "What happened?"

Chip relayed the events, keeping it short to lessen the embarrassment. Garth looked over at Chase, who met his gaze and then looked down sullenly. The weapons master said nothing.

"What is done is done. Learn from it, and do not make the same mistake again," the wizard said, resting his hand on the boy's burnt arm.

Blue fire erupted in his eyes, and Chip felt a tickling sensation run up his wrist. The melted skin reformed until only a slight pinkness remained. The wizard opened his eyes and nodded. "That should do it." The boy thanked him.

Xander waved it off and pointed at the line. "We've already processed two times that many people. The army is growing rapidly. City workers inside are scrambling to find food and clothes and assign duties to everyone. Messenger pigeons were sent to Toron, Calgar, and the Guild, explaining how Banfar would assist the war effort. Guards are combing the Lower District for hidden Dark Elves, but I suspect you have killed most of them. The one who got away is long gone."

At that moment, a guard galloped up to them and reigned in his mount before the table. "General Morris," he saluted. Chip blinked at the title. Captain Morris had been promoted. "A cloaked figure on horseback burned a front gate guard with green fire and forced the other to open the gates. He galloped west towards the mountains." Morris looked up at Xander.

The wizard sighed. "Nothing we can do about it, General. I have no magic wielders to send after the Dark Elf. A contingent of guards would only get hurt if they tried to catch him." He waved his hand. "Let him go. I will guarantee there are still humans here who would betray us and relay information to the other side. Bring the front gate guard here for healing."

The general looked at the soldier. "Replace the gatekeeper and expand the search from the Lower District to the entire city. I want to make sure there is not a single Dark Elf left in this town." The guard saluted and left. Morris looked at Captain Melvin. "I am assigning your company to provide security for the Guardian and his companions."

He turned to Chip. "I could try and ban the crowds from following you, but honestly, I have never seen the city so full of hope. The people of Banfar finally have someone and something to rally behind. We are the outcasts of society. Here congregates the fringes of humanity. We house the homeless, the shunned, the addicts, the criminals, and the banished. Even the guards end up here from other cities or posts, usually for various derelictions of duty or plain punishment. A change has swept over Banfar because you showed them that something good still exists in this world. Instead of giving up and joining evil, they can fight it. You are the orphan turned Guardian. In a way, you represent them all. Therefore, I hope you will allow the crowds to see you. We will protect you with our lives. Captain Melvin and his company are my most trusted soldiers. Is this acceptable, Mr. Guardian?"

Everyone looked at Chip, waiting for his response. At first, he wanted to tell the general to keep the crowds away because he didn't want to endanger his friends again. Yet, as he listened to the man's impassioned plea, the boy realized that he, a lowly orphan, could make a difference after all.

It was a difficult concept for his mind to comprehend. He had always considered himself an outcast, something nobody wanted, not even his parents. His best hope was to become a common soldier with fair treatment and not be shunned for being a demon or orphan. King Barton wanted to banish him, and Rupert wished to sentence him to life as a perpetual scullery boy in the kitchen.

The weapons master always taught him to be grateful even for the smallest of life's blessings, and he found great solace in that. Though he lived in a horse's stable, the orphan was grateful for the little stall he called 'home.' It usually smelled of horse manure, had vicious cold drafts in winter, and reverberated with a constant clatter of horse noise, but it was his.

Others were homeless and had no one. They were not as fortunate. His training and schooling were more than an orphan could ever hope for. The boy was used to being hated and scorned. His red eyes and orphan heritage were heavy burdens, but Garth would say they were his challenges.

To have Eleanor and Chase, a princess and squire's son, as his best friends was nothing short of amazing. For a cast-out orphan like him, it was a fairy tale. Chip remembered how he would pray nightly as a young boy, thanking the Creator that he had found friends, let alone ones of such stature. Even a famous wizard was willing to acknowledge him. He did not think it could get any better.

For a long time, he constantly dreaded that it would all crash around him. They did not owe him anything. The only way he could repay their kindness was to try his hardest in training and school. His greatest fear was that he would disappoint them. Yet day after day, even when he made a mistake in training or did not understand something in school, they gave him another chance. They did not banish him or kick him out onto the streets. They were his real friends and stood by him.

General Morris and his guards were all looking at him. He was being asked to be a beacon of hope for the people, including all the orphans, outcasts, and unfortunate ones. The boy took a deep breath. It was then that Chip realized his true purpose. He vowed never to give up on people, including the orphans and outcasts. After all, his friends never gave up on him.

If he were lucky enough to be a person who could inspire hope and change in others, then he would do so with the greatest humility, despite the risk. He knew that if he did not honestly believe in his own worthiness, he would be unable to inspire it in others. The orphan allowed himself to believe he was worthy of such a role. It was a monumental shift in his thinking.

Chip faced the general. "It would be an honour, sir. I will be their Guardian."

9

The gravity of the boy's words was such that the general stood and saluted. All the soldiers watching did the same. "Thank you, Guardian. You give us all hope." Xander smiled. The weapons master looked at him with pride. He then did something that Chip never would have imagined.

Garth Stone turned to the boy and saluted. "I, as High Commander of Vanalon, Honorary High Commander of Toron, Master Trainer of the Guild, and Protector of the Grand Wizard Xandrostika, decree and bestow upon you the new office of Guardian of Humanity, second only to High King Dominor and High Wizard Balor." The boy's eyes widened. "Do I have a second?"

Xander stepped forward, back straight. "I, Grand Wizard Xandrostika of the Guild, Senior Advisor to High King Dominor of Toron, Taker of the Orb of Power, and Peacemaker of the Races, bestow and bind the position of Guardian of Humanity upon you, Chip..." He turned and whispered something in Garth's ear. The weapons master nodded. Xander continued, "Oathbinder."

He turned to the guards and the people in line. Raising his voice, the wizard proclaimed, "Whoever fights for the light will swear an oath to Chip Oathbinder, Guardian of Humanity." He turned to the boy. "I, Grand Wizard Xandrostika, swear an oath to pledge my allegiance to the Guardian of Humanity and defend humankind."

The rest of the crowd turned and as one repeated the oath. The wizard took a knee, followed by all the soldiers and the entire crowd, facing the Guardian. There was complete silence as the people waited on Chip Oathbinder, who looked around in awe. For a moment, it was almost too overwhelming, but he remembered his training and found the Calm. He knew they wanted him to speak and reminded himself that he could make a difference.

In a loud, clear voice, he spoke to those gathered. "I accept the position of Guardian of Humanity with humility and reverence. It is the highest honour. You have pledged allegiance not only to me but to humanity. I bind you all to your oath. We must fight as one to defeat this evil. A great darkness is coming, and we must be the light. I fight for all that is good in the world. May the Creator bless us all. Please rise. I would ask that you not kneel before me. After all, I am not the Creator. A bow or a salute is more than enough to respect the position, and even that I will never enforce. However, I consider myself a binder of oaths and hold you to it. Fight with me, and together, we will prevail."

He pointed one finger at the sky in salute. Cheers erupted all around. His companions clapped him on the back. The princess leaned forward and kissed his cheek.

"You might be a natural," she whispered in his ear, smiling.

"I'm trying not to shake," he admitted.

The weapons master walked up to Chase, who looked sullen.

"Why the long face?" he asked.

Chase looked down. "I failed to protect them."

"No, you made a mistake and learned from it. Will you be more vigilant after this?" Chase nodded. "Good, then hold your head up high." Garth looked at Chip. "May I bestow one more position?" The boy nodded, not sure what he meant.

The weapons master turned back to Chase. "I, Garth Stone, Master Trainer of the Guild, bestow the title of Interim Protector of the Guardian of Humanity on you, Chase Longfellow. It can only be officially bestowed at the Wizard's Guild if you pass the Tests, of course, but somehow, I think you will do fine." He smiled. "Do you accept the position?"

Chase looked around as everyone turned to stare at him. He blushed and tried to hide his pride.

"Yes, sir. Someone's got to protect this skinny orphan." Several guards opened their mouths in shock and then relaxed as the Guardian laughed.

"I will accept his protection, but if he fails those Tests, I want a new one," Chip smirked and saluted his best friend. "We've got a lot of work to do." The boy turned to the general. "If it's alright with you, I would like to go with the guards and help them ferret out any remaining Dark Elves. I cannot sense them with my magic unless they are using their Power, but I can at least tell where hidden life forms exist. I want to clear the city of this infestation."

The general bowed his head. "I take orders from you, Guardian, not the other way around. Please do as you see fit. Captain Melvin and his contingent are at your disposal. If you need anything else, do not hesitate."

"Thank you. I would ask that the gate guards require anyone who wishes to enter the city to remove their hoods to ensure they are not Dark Elves."

"At once, Guardian." The general saluted.

Xander looked at Chip appraisingly. "Good start, lad. You will grow into the position. Let us do everything we can today to prepare the city. I want to leave by lunchtime tomorrow. If we delay any longer, we risk attack by those who surely follow. At least on the plains, we can see it coming. The trackers will be here soon."

Chip nodded then looked at Captain Melvin. "Please take me to the guards who are searching the city. I can assist."

"Um, hello," Chase interjected, raising his hand. "I'm hungry."

Chip remembered the silver coin in his pocket. He laughed. "Alright, food first, Captain, then please take me to the guards."

Captain Melvin saluted. "At once, Guardian." They turned and mounted their horses.

Chip rode beside the princess, surrounded by the phalanx of guards. He leaned over. "I'm not sure I can get used to this Guardian stuff."

She laughed.

"Now you know how it feels to be a princess, Your Highness."

His eyes bulged. "Huh, a Guardian is not a Highness, is he?" the boy asked incredulously. She laughed loud and pure. Some of the guards raised their eyebrows.

"No, silly. I was joking."

"Oh," he said relieved.

"Actually, I am not sure. You are now above everyone but High King Dominor and High Wizard Balor, so I guess you are a Highness." She started laughing again.

"But I have no kingdom," he pointed out.

"In theory, you represent all the land of humankind."

He looked at her, trying to determine whether she was serious. The princess tried to hide a giggle. Chip snorted, "You know what? I do not care anyway. I'm just going to be me."

She laughed even harder. "Good luck with that. The higher the privilege, the higher the duty, remember?" He rolled his eyes. They had talked about that the night before. Her laughter became too infectious to resist, so he finally joined in.

Captain Melvin took the group to a tavern off the main strip and assured them the lamb stew was the best in town. Chip realized how famished he was. They ended up sitting out front surrounded by guards. Three heaping bowls arrived with an accompanying mug of ale. Chip dug in and had to admit it was the best lamb he ever tasted. As they ate, people gathered around to see what the commotion was. Soon, a crowd formed, pointing at the boy and waving.

"All hail the Guardian," one of them called out. Others followed suit. Chip sighed.

"Get used to it," the princess said. "In the end, you might wish you were ordinary again." He sighed, then expressed gratitude to the owner, trying to put a silver coin in his hand.

"Thank you, that was delicious," he said.

"Your money is no good here, Mr. Guardian," the tavern owner said. "It was an honour to serve you."

"Oh no, please take it," Chip said, trying again.

"No, Mr. Guardian, I insist. I will tell my kids and grandkids that the Guardian of Humanity ate at my establishment. Please keep your money." The man bowed low and left. The boy looked at Eleanor, who was covering her smile, and then stared at the silver coin in his hand.

"I finally got money for the first time in my life, and now I can't spend it." Chip threw up his hands.

The princess laughed. "When you need it most, it is hard to get, but when you do not, you have it." Chase was about to comment then sat back, trying to follow her remark.

Chip sighed. "So true. Let's go. This crowd is getting too big for my liking."

Captain Melvin escorted them through the gathering throng to the middle of the Lower District. It had taken all morning for the inspection guards to work their way up from the gates to that point, trying to ferret out any more Dark Elves. The captain talked to the lead guard, named Herman, and informed him that Chip would assist.

Herman looked at them sourly. His shirt was stained, and a smell of whiskey wafted off him. "Is this necessary?" he asked, scratching himself between the legs. Eleanor turned away. Chase was scanning the crowd for potential threats but glanced at the man with a dark look. Captain Melvin was about to comment when Chip pushed his horse before the man. He broke through his Wall, eyes blazing bright red. Herman shrank back in fear, itches forgotten.

The boy leaned down. "It is not necessary for you. I relieve you of duty until you sober up, wash your uniform, learn the chain of command, and ask to be retrained." Chip dismissed him.

The guard's fear turned into anger. "You do not order me around,

Mr... whatever they call you. I was working this city when you weren't even born." Herman belched and tried to grab something to lean on, swaying. "I oughtta... teach you some manners."

His face was suddenly full of dirt as Captain Melvin leapt off his horse and slammed the man into the ground. He signalled for two others to grab Herman's arms.

"Put him in the hole until he sobers up." The guards complied, pulling the drunken man to his feet and escorting him away. Of the twenty or so soldiers left on the inspection team, another five were ordered to clean up and get sober.

"Let's start at the gates again," Chip said. "I do not trust Herman did a thorough enough job. The captain nodded, and they followed him to the front gates. They turned around and methodically searched the Lower District. Chip sent out his magic to each building and identified the number of life forms in each home. Some had none, and they did not need to go inside. They were halfway back to where they started when Chip felt the peculiar crackle of magic. This time, he wrapped the three of them in a red shield. Green fire struck him on the shoulder, doing no harm.

Filled with Power, the boy followed the green line and pulled the Dark Elf straight through the window of a two-story building. The sign was missing from the store below, indicating it had once had a symbol on it. The elf hung suspended in midair, surrounded by a red hand of Power. He looked at Chip with hate-filled eyes and gnashed his teeth.

"We are coming for you, boy," the Dark Elf hissed with malevolence. Chip considered trying to wring information out of this evil being, but he knew the elf would lie. The boy was not convinced he had any helpful knowledge anyway.

Chip decided to put it to the test. "Why are you in Banfar?"

The Dark Elf sneered. "To save humans when my Master arrives, may we grovel at his leisure."

"Why are you really here?"

The elf spat, "I told you." A crowd had gathered, watching the spectacle. Some whispered that the Dark Elf might be speaking the truth.

"Tell them the real truth," Chip said, pointing to the crowd. "If you do, I will release you unhindered." The Dark Elf looked at him for a moment.

"You lie," he hissed.

"I do not. Unlike you, I am a man of my word. You can walk out the front gates unscathed, and I will order everyone to stand down. We will not follow you," the boy promised.

The elf considered. "For what purpose?" he asked, apparently trying to gather more information. His green eyes blazed, but he did not try to resist.

"I want you to tell the people the truth for once. To your Master, you can say whatever you want. I will only offer this to you alone. Any other Dark Elf I find, I will kill. I do not understand why you would disagree. Surely, your demon army can take this small city."

"We will take all cities," he answered savagely.

"You must not be sure of that if you need converts. Are you afraid that without followers, you cannot take the small town of Banfar?" the boy asked.

"We do not need these pathetic converts." The Dark Elf looked around with contempt. "Very well. It matters not anyway. The city offers certain pleasures that only an inferior human race can provide. The followers would have made the city fall easier, but this cesspool will stand no chance against my Master anyway, may we grovel at his leisure." He raised his voice. "The truth is the pathetic humans who join our cause will be enslaved. We will use our followers for various pleasures and torture them until the end of their lives. Our pets will feed on them piece by piece..." He giggled madly.

The crowd started grumbling and yelling out epithets.

"You lied to me!" a woman screamed.

"I trusted you!" a man yelled.

"Hope you burn, you evil monster!"

"May the Creator strike you down!"

"The Guardian will save us!"

The Dark Elf chuckled, looking at Chip. "Guardian? Is that what they call you now?" His laugh turned into a cackle. "You may be strong for a human, but my king has grown into a living god." He looked at the crowd and extended his long tongue, licking his lips. "You weak humans are not worthy to kiss my Master's feet. I will be back to watch my pets eat your flesh," he spat. "Now release me, Guardian of Nothing." The people started screaming for his death.

"Don't release him!"

"Let's get him!"

"We will tear him apart!"

Chip raised his hands to the crowd. "I did this to prove that you have been deceived. The price was allowing him to live. Trust me, it is a small price to save even one human life. I gave my word to release him, and I will keep it. I am called Oathbinder for a reason. Go back to the time in your life when your word meant something. Become that person again." He turned to the Dark Elf. "You will be released unharmed. No one will follow you but mark my words. If I ever see you again, you will die." He paused, and the crowd went silent.

"One more thing." Chip looked at the Dark Elf, remembering the human bones in Cave Mountain, and his voice filled with rage. "Tell your Master, as the Creator is my witness, the Guardian is coming for him."

The boy levitated the Dark Elf higher, causing him to shriek in fear. Then, with unimaginable speed, he cast him over the gates and set him down on his feet. The crowd watched the display of pure power and began cheering.

Chip turned to Captain Melvin. "Let's continue the search." The man nodded and led them to the next store. This continued until they reached the place with the horned helmet. The boy wore a grim expression, remembering the princess tied to the altar. Eleanor's features hardened, but she held her head up.

The sign was gone, and the store stood empty. The boy extended his presence, not expecting to find anything, especially in this location, and began to withdraw. But something stopped him.

Chip felt a tugging coming from the basement behind the altar. It was so faint that he almost missed it. He stopped, then turned and walked into the store. The guards followed. The crowd started murmuring excitedly, hoping they would witness more fireworks. He strode to the back of the store and down the steps. Chase and Eleanor followed close behind. They saw his look of concentration and did not disturb him. Chip reached the cavernous room deep underground and immediately smelt death and blood. The bodies were gone, but large stains covered the rock floor. He sent out his magic and gasped. The boy sensed life forms in a large, hidden room behind the altar. There were people in the room, lots of them. He looked at the soldiers. "Prepare yourself."

Chase pulled his sword, and the guards did the same.

"What is it?" asked the captain.

The Guardian put a finger to his lips and whispered. "There is a large room behind the back wall." He went up to the stone and sent his magic out. He could find no opening. Chip decided to try going downwards and immediately found a tunnel directly underneath him leading to stairs. He turned around, his gaze settling on the altar. "There," he signalled to the guards. "Help me push." They did so, but the altar would not budge. They tried pushing it from the other side, and this time, it moved easily, revealing a large, black, rectangular hole.

Distant cries and screams sounded from below. They handed him a torch. He looked at the princess, who took a deep breath and followed him down the stairs. After ten steps, the boy entered a tunnel that extended underneath the back wall of the cavernous room. They crept down the tunnel cautiously, seeing stairs at the end. A foul smell assaulted them as they edged forward.

Chip handed off the torch to one of the guards and began ascending the steps, not knowing what to expect. The cries grew louder. When the boy reached the top of the stairs, horror greeted him.

Chip had seen many despicable things in his young life, yet even those did not prepare him for this. They entered a vast stone room where demons sat around in a circle, chewing noisily on human remains. One was crunching on a small arm while another picked a ribcage clean. Other half-eaten body parts were strewn about the chamber.

Humans of all ages stood shackled to rings lining the walls on both sides. Some cried out in pain, holding bitten-off appendages. Others were dead, their flesh hanging like rotting meat. Bite marks covered their bodies, leaving gaping holes reeking of infection. Most were in a stupor, unable to process they were missing arms and legs. Even as they watched, a clawed demon stepped up to an old man chained to the wall, lifted his hand, and bit his fingers off. Chip pushed back his nausea, and his rage ignited.

Then he saw an old Dark Elf lying on a plush divan at the back of the room. Half-naked people surrounded him, some missing arms and legs, ready to fulfill his every whim. The smell was unbearable. One of the guards behind him gagged, spewing vomit on the floor. The Dark Elf's head whipped up, and his black eyes blazed bright blue. The demons lurched to their feet, mewling and shrieking at the prospect of new food. Chip's eyes flared red, giving them pause. They had never seen a human like him.

"Get them!" screamed the old elf in a hoarse voice. The demons fanned out and ran forward. Chip had to be careful not to hit any surviving humans with his magic. His instinct was to grab his sword, but that would be too merciful for these foul creatures. He wanted to burn them.

The boy lifted both hands, and red fire exploded into the first two demons. Giant holes appeared in their chests as they fell in smoking heaps, faces locked in shock. A third ran around to lunge at Chase, who greeted the demon with a swift thrust of his sword, driving the tip through the beast's chin and out the back of its head. The Dark Elf, watching his pets fall, unleashed a substantial blue fireball that barreled towards the boy. Chip formed a thick shield, absorbing it, then strode forward. The elf looked at him shrewdly.

Captain Melvin and three guards surrounded a short, stocky demon with horns, stabbing it simultaneously until it stopped moving. Eleanor threw out brown-pointed magic daggers, impaling a fat, slow demon until it leaked black blood and deflated like a rotten melon. The last demon's head flew off as Chase executed a mighty swing. Weak cries sounded from the humans chained to the wall.

The old Dark Elf stood up fully naked. He had a ponderous belly and skin covered by odd lesions. He grabbed a scantily clad woman and held her in front of him. "Now, now," he said, raising an empty palm. "I will melt her if you come closer." Chip stopped in the middle of the room, trying not to look at the body parts around his feet. He trembled with rage.

"What are you?" the boy asked with disgust.

"Well, I was Inner Circle long ago," he answered, laughing with a hoarse bellow as a frog might. "My name is Bashan. I was there long before the barrier. Killian stripped me of my rank when I dared to question his decision on a matter. He tortured me for a few centuries then felt a change of heart and allowed me to wash his feet. This went on for a couple of thousand years, give or take. When the barrier weakened a few months ago, I volunteered to go first, and he agreed, for old time's sake, as you humans say. I decided not to serve him anymore and came to Banfar."

"Why would you do...this?" Chip looked at the room in horror.

The Dark Elf looked around and then gazed at the boy sadly. The emotion surprised even him. "The Power changed us, corrupted us. We took down our Walls permanently, and our eyes grew dark. Morgo taught us how to do it. I was there when Killian changed. You see, I was his childhood friend. His Power is much stronger than mine, so he ages far less."

His blazing eyes seemed to grow distant, remembering millennia ago. "We made the wrong choice and succumbed to our darkest desires. The Power caused a hunger in us for death and destruction. We captured humans after the Breaking and did unspeakable things to them. Behind the barrier, Morgo found ways to harness more magic for his Master. Killian became mad with Power. He tortured me relentlessly for hundreds of years. My mind fragmented, and I became a creature that only desired to hurt others. I nursed my hatred of him and directed it at humans."

He looked at the woman in front of him, squeezing her neck. She cried out in pain.

"To me, she is an object of pleasure. I enjoy her suffering. I want everyone to suffer as I did." He stared at Chip with eyes devoid of emotion yet still full of hunger. "I have some of the Telling. I knew you were coming. I will die at your hands, boy. I have been waiting for you for a long time. I thought you would find me last night when you were saving your princess on the altar in the adjoining cavern. You killed Spider, my favourite little disciple. He led many humans to me, many...treats. He would have become like me."

He stoked the woman's hair in front of him, watching her shudder. "They call you the Guardian. You have done much in a short time. When I heard Morgo was dead, I rejoiced. Elohan was a pompous ass, and Marta was too controlling. All of them deserved it. What you did in Cave Mountain was impressive."

Chip looked up sharply. "How could you know that?"

Bashan noticed the reaction and smiled evilly. "I have many eyes and ears. I felt the magic from here. You may have buried the Dim, but Killian will release it. He will use it to upset the balance further." Bashan paused, looking down at the pouch by Chip's waist. Understanding lit his eyes. "Ah, I see. You found it. That is how you did it." He nodded knowingly, his respect for the boy seeming to grow. "She will be a powerful ally. We believe the dragons were created as the balance to the Dim. When Killian reveals the Great Forget, all will become clear."

"What do you know of the Great Forget?"

Bashan chuckled grossly. The movement caused some of the pustules protruding from his body to leak. The smell was nauseating. "A millennia before the Breaking, five thousand years ago, a great magic was unleashed on the world. We believe this world was called Earth, even before the Great Forget. A name etched in everyone's memory would be difficult to erase with any magic. Perhaps other city names or at least a variation of them remained the same. The land itself may have shifted or altered.

"Morgo existed in a small fishing village at the time and became altered. The Dim and the dragons came into being, among others. The troll Barko was only a boy but a curious one who unearthed the Dark Arts. Later, he would make bargains that would change the world. Many species and races, perhaps even elves and humans, came into being, but no one knows who existed first.

"When Killian entered the Ancient City of the Red-Eyed King, he almost found the answers. He said that something about the city itself gave clues, but even that faded with memory as he left. No humans or elves could create a magic of such Power, not even with the orb. The book in the ancient library will tell us who created the Great Forgot. Yet only when one red-eye is left."

He paused, studying the boy with an unreadable expression as he considered his next words.

"That means the Red-Eyed King alone guards the secrets. Who is he? Figure that out, and you may have your answer. My Telling says there is still a Path from you to him, but many do not lead there. The Dim has already changed much. Each person it touches alters the Paths like a spider web. When too many strands disappear, the web collapses. If you faced the Demon King right now, he would crush you. Then again, no human has ever had Power like yours. You are the balance to Killian, but he has...broken the rules and cheated. One force even assists him...bending everything further. The Demon King is set to wipe out everything, not only you but all the races. He will ride his black dragon across a demon world empty of life. Those foul creatures will finally die without sustenance, leaving the Demon King to rule over a dead Earth. He is mad." Bashan looked around the room, seeing the tortured humans as if for the first time. "As am I."

"How do I stop him? How can I kill the Demon King?"

The old Dark Elf looked at him, and his eyes grew unfocused. "I See my last Telling. You are going to kill me soon." He shuddered with what appeared to be ecstasy. "I have waited so long."

He made a purring sound as a cat would if pet behind the ears. His grotesque body jiggled, releasing more pus. His eyes seemed to clear, and he looked straight at Chip then bellowed hoarsely, "Ha, perhaps I am the vessel the Balance will use. I may have a purpose, after all. I cannot tell you much, but it may be enough. Find the Light Elves, boy. Talk to King Luminor. He still lives... He knows you." The Dark Elf looked confused then shrugged. "His location is shrouded in darkness, but the answer lies in the wizard histories. Look through them all." He paused and stared at the princess. "She will die." Chip's heart sank. He almost lost control of his Power.

"There must be another way," he insisted.

"Oh, there is," Bashan said with a lecherous grin. "But it would guarantee the end of the world. You could hide her somewhere safe until the Last Battle is over, but you would lose, and she would die anyway. Humanity has only a small chance of victory, and it is through her death. After that, I cannot See. Oh, and the wizard already knows." Chip looked up in disbelief. Bashan chortled. Flecks of spittle appeared on his cracked lips. "Yes, it's true. The Orb Stealer knows. Did he not tell you?"

Chip looked at him in rage, his eyes blazing. "You lie!" he screamed.

The reaction caused the Dark Elf to bellow uproariously. "Ha, even upon my death, I can still feel enormous pleasure from another's pain. Yours tastes as sweet as I ever had. You will suffer like the rest of us, Guardian of Humanity. This thing called life spares no one. I have no love for humans, but I hate you less than my former Master. I would see Killian lose to a mere boy."

He chuckled again, the sound of phlegm intermixing in his chest.

"Any last words before you die?" Chip asked menacingly, stepping forward.

Bashan stared at him. "Yes. You must face the Red-Eyed King." He sighed and released the girl. "I have played my part."

With a look of mad pleasure, his eyes blazed brighter blue, and he shot his full Power at the orphan. Chip raised his hands and blocked it. The Dark Elf's face contorted as he threw all his magic at the shield. Gritting his teeth, he grunted, "I do not wish to face all the souls I have put in the afterlife. Let us see how strong you really are, Guardian."

His eyes suddenly blazed white, and with shock, Chip realized

Bashan was attacking him with his spirit essence. The boy pulled in more Power and reinforced his shield. A ball of pure white light shot out of the Dark Elf, slamming into his shield and sending Chip hurtling backwards into the guards. They held him up as the red shield buckled then consumed the white light.

The boy stood up and watched in amazement as Bashan's body disappeared. His spirit essence contained all of him, including his physical form. He now ceased to exist, devoid of life forever.

10

"Release them," Chip ordered, pointing at the people chained to the wall. "Get any healers and magic wielders throughout the city."

He ran up to one child, still chained. She was very young and had a deep bite mark on her shoulder. He held her hand, healed the injury, cupped her cheek and smiled. "It is over now. They won't hurt you anymore. Be strong."

The boy went to the other children first and then to the most grievously injured adults. Eleanor did the same, using her brown magic to mend bones and regrow limbs. Other magic wielders entered and began helping. Their magic was much weaker, mostly untrained Yellows and one lesser Brown, but they made a difference.

When finished, Chip sank back wearily. All the significant injuries were healed. Two victims were beyond saving, and a third died as he tried to heal him. The man was essentially a body with no limbs, already on his way to the afterlife. Eleanor sat beside the boy, exhausted.

He looked at her, and the full force of the Telling sunk in. Bashan had predicted her death and did it in the manner of a confession, leaving little doubt that at least he believed it to be accurate. Chip dropped his head, finding it difficult to talk. The idea of a world without her was overwhelming.

She put her head on his shoulder and patted his arm. "It's alright. I have lived a short but great life. I got to meet you, after all. Look at these people. Think of what they have gone through. There is so much suffering in this world. If, by my death, I can relieve suffering, then I will give it."

She looked at him and raised his chin. A large tear slowly slid down his cheek. "Did we really think this would be easy and we would live happily ever after? If we fail, we all die anyway, and some will experience unspeakable suffering. You are the Guardian of Humanity. Remember what we talked about. The higher the privilege, the higher the duty. We must think of others. This is where it gets hard. It was never about us, Chip. We are responsible for everyone. As a princess, I am responsible for the people of Vanalon. They come first. For the Guardian, humanity comes first. If the path to saving everyone leads through my death, that is the way." She kissed him on the lips, then giggled. "Besides, he never said when I will die. Let us enjoy the time we have left." He hugged her impulsively, not letting go.

"I love you," she whispered in his ear and kissed him again.

"I love you too," he said thickly.

"I know." She smiled, wiped the tears from his green eyes, and then fixed his hair. "Nothing worth anything is ever easy. My mom used to say that. I will wait for you in the afterlife, Chip Oathbinder. Until then, let's stir things up, shall we?"

She laughed infectiously, and he had no choice but to join in. They stood up, and Chase ambled over. He looked at the princess with a glum look.

"I'm sorry," he said. "If I can stop it, I will."

She hugged him. "My destiny is set. When it happens, protect Chip. He is the only one who can save us." She smiled and patted Chase's cheek. "I think we have some time yet, so let us not dwell on this anymore. We still have to finish sweeping the Lower District, then we can find another good place to dine. My favourite is chicken."

Chase rubbed his stomach. "Chicken sounds fine to me."

She grabbed both their hands and led them out of the cavern. The last of the human victims were taken to a healing center. The blood, gore, and stench remained, but at least the physical suffering was over. Now that the old Dark Elf was dead, the air seemed to change. The great evil that was Bashan was gone from the world forever.

Captain Melvin led the way. "Should we escort you back to the Reindeer Inn, my Lord Guardian?"

"No, let us continue sweeping the Lower District. We can finish by this evening, and then we would love to eat a good chicken meal," Chip said with a tired smile.

"Yes, sir. I know just the spot." They exited the store, breathing in the fresh air. The crowd had swelled even further as word of the torture chamber spread like wildfire. Shouts of "Hail the Guardian" rang out. After witnessing the Dark Elf's confession and watching the tortured humans exiting the store, it was now clear to the crowd what the Demon King's intentions were. The news would spread, and Banfar would learn who the real enemy was.

"Allow tours of the torture chambers for those in the crowd who are still in doubt," Chip instructed. Melvin immediately assigned two guards to coordinate the viewings. "No one can ever deny it after seeing what's below. Let's carry on."

They continued searching stores as the guards surrounded them in a circle, keeping the crowd at bay. The people, for the most part, understood they had work to do, so they did not try to press forward. The air was one of friendliness and realization. A feeling of hope permeated the city, which had been absent in Banfar for a long time. They reached the end of the Lower District faster than anticipated, finding no more Dark Elves.

"Can we please eat now?" Chase lamented, causing the other two to laugh.

"Yes, my dear Protector. I will give you food to make you big and strong," Chip said in a deep voice. He turned to Captain Melvin, smiling. "Take us to good chicken, kind sir."

The captain returned the smile and nodded. "Follow me, ladies and gents." He spurred his horse forward. With a final wave to the crowd, the companions followed. Soon after, the noise died down. The sun was slipping behind the mountains to the west. It had been a long day, but they knew they had saved lives, so it was well worth it.

The trio ate at a small place in the Upper District, entering with their heads down before too many people recognized them. Chip did not realize that being famous came with so many strings attached. Most of the guards remained outside as Captain Melvin brought them to the back of the quaint restaurant. Several couples, eating quietly over candles, looked up in shock, recognizing him as the Guardian.

The captain asked them politely to leave, but Chip told them to stay.

"I may be the Guardian, but that does not mean I cannot eat with the good people of Banfar. Let them stay, Captain."

"But your safety, sir?" Melvin said, looking around apprehensively.

Chip laughed. "I have a Protector, remember."

Melvin looked at Chase's large frame and nodded. "Very well. Let me introduce you to the owner."

The companions met Tarn, a small man who had been a chicken farmer turned restaurateur, who insisted they try the bird in various ways. He served them succulent chicken pieces in a rich bone broth, followed by a platter with the bird roasted, fried, battered, and stewed. They all agreed it was better than anything Miss Stern and her cooks could make. When finished, they thanked the owner and said goodbye to the gawking patrons. They asked Captain Melvin to take them back to the inn so they could wash up and retire.

A short while later, they arrived at the Reindeer Inn. Chip led the trio to Xander's room and knocked loudly. The weapons master let them in, and he sat down quickly in front of the wizard.

"I heard you had quite the day," Xander said, looking at them with concern. "Are you alright?"

Chip replayed the old Dark Elf's Telling in his mind and tried to control his anger. "Did you know she was going to die?" he said without preamble.

Xander's eyes widened, and he glanced at the weapons master. "Who told you this?"

"That is not what I asked. Did you know?" he repeated louder.

"Yes."

Chip gritted his teeth. "Why didn't you tell me?"

"Because it would have changed the prophecy."

"What do you mean?" Chip did not expect that answer.

The wizard sat back, sighing. He pulled out his pipe and put in a small amount of tobacco, pondering carefully. Chip restrained himself, trying to find the Calm. Eleanor reached over and rubbed his back.

Xander noticed the boy's discomfort. "There is a powerful prophecy from a young wizard named Skylar over three millennia ago. Grand Wizard Skylar is now quite frankly an old curmudgeon past his prime, to put it lightly." The wizard lit his pipe and took a long pull. "To be fair, he was the greatest human Teller of his time. The problem with prophecy is that we do not know which one is true until events narrow things down. If a Teller comes up with ten prophecies, one event could eliminate five in one fell swoop. What makes this prophecy so powerful is that everything has come true since it was foretold over three thousand years ago. It talks of a red-eyed boy who will challenge the Demon King and provide a balance to a gross misuse of Power. This boy would link with a dragon, become the Guardian of Humanity, and love a princess..."

He paused, his face growing sad. "The princess would die. If any human warned the boy of her impending death, then the prophecy would fold in on itself, and humanity would fall. So, to answer your question, yes, I knew. I could not tell you because it would likely end the world. We also reasoned that if the prophecy was not true, then telling you would amount to nothing anyway."

Chip looked at him, his anger disappearing. "Is it possible the prophecy is wrong?"

"Yes," Xander answered.

"Are there other prophecies?" Chip asked with a note of excitement.

"Yes."

"So why can't they be true?"

"They are much vaguer. This prophecy has been very specific from the beginning. It is considered a Core Prophecy. The others that do not lead up to it have been discarded. I personally believe free will can change what is predicted. It is a constant philosophical discussion in the Guild and by learned humans throughout history. Is there really free will? Or are we forever slaves to our human makeup and environment? Do we have a choice in anything? I side with the proponents of freedom. The other option is too unsettling. Yet, even given our freedom to choose, events can lead us down certain paths that are very difficult to avoid. In that sense, we cannot choose and must ride the tides of fate. Many events we cannot control, no matter how much we wish. Can you change when a mountain erupts, the timing of the tides, or even an irrational person?

"So far, this prophecy has held true. Tellers will now speak of Paths in the future from this new starting point. Again, many will not materialize. I point to free will, which eliminates many of the Paths, which the other side believes is an illusion. To them, there are no choices or, at most, predetermined choices that appear as if we chose them. Remember, Tellers have a wide range of skills, and many allow their human biases or interpretation to colour their visions. Many cannot See the full version, so instead, they talk of pieces or fragmented visions that can be out of sequence. Many disjointed prophecies are taken out of context to bolster someone's ego. Worse, the risk of a self-fulfilling prophecy is ever-present. If I receive a vision whereby a king is assassinated and then commit the act myself, is the prophecy not proven true?"

"So this may not come to pass," Chip said hopefully.

"It may not. However, it has been correct for three thousand years.

It ends with her death, no matter which branch you take. Unfortunately, it is not the only prophecy that speaks of this. Now that an old Dark Elf is saying it after having a recent Telling is frightening. That, more than anything, is what disturbs me."

"What do you mean? I thought it was one prophecy," the boy asked with a furrowed brow.

"Right now, we are at a nexus. Think of it like a nodule with branches leading to it and branches leading away. This Core Prophecy so far has had no branches until now. That is quite rare. That is why it is so powerful. Other prophecies usually have many branches or Paths, so when an event happens, the false branches are eliminated. With many Tellers, they only see one branch or one nexus and then try to collaborate to put the pieces together. That is where many errors can occur. When an event eliminates all branches, the prophecy is declared dead. Tellers or Seers do not like to call them failed prophecies because it implies they have no magic or are untrustworthy. They say instead that free will changed fate or that the Balance created new Paths. The greatest proponents of free will are, ironically, the Tellers themselves. It allows them to be wrong."

"I'm still confused. How can all branches lead to her death?"

"I'm getting to that." The wizard took another pull on his pipe. "The first nexus in this Core Prophecy by Skylar occurs when you are called the Guardian of Humanity."

"But you called me that."

Xander grimaced. "Strictly speaking, Garth did, but I admit I announced it to everyone." He raised his palms upwards. "It felt right at the time."

"But that means you caused the prophecy to happen. You made it self-fulfilling," Chip accused him, growing angry again.

"Well, my goodness. Maybe there is no free will after all. All I know is that I was introducing you to the crowd and giving you all those titles, which felt like the correct thing to do. The real question is whether I would have called you the Guardian of Humanity if I had never read the prophecy or heard the name. I would have used the other names, but I am unsure about 'Guardian.' I will say that the prophecy was not in my mind then. I prefer to focus on actual events, not prophecies, for that very reason.

"In this case, I fulfilled it. This may point to prophecy itself being a necessary component of fate, which is disturbing. It could again be an illusion of free will, which fate uses to do exactly what it wants. I would prefer not to consider the implications. The point is we are now at the nexus. This prophecy branches, but even if you try to hide the princess, in the end, she dies anyway. The only difference is doing something like that will guarantee the rest of us die too."

Chip felt a chill go through his body. That was precisely what the evil old Dark Elf said. The boy sighed. All this talk of prophecy was making his head hurt.

"Bashan said the same thing," he admitted.

"Ah, Bashan," the wizard said softly. "I know of him. While you were eating chicken in that lovely restaurant, word spread like wildfire of an old Dark Elf torturing humans and you stopped him. The people of Banfar have now turned from their old beliefs about the Demon King and stand behind you." He nodded in approval. "You are too harsh on yourself. You have done great things here, necessary things. If I was an unwitting catalyst, so be it. These events have saved many lives."

Chip leaned forward. "I will save her too," he said with deadly conviction. The princess put her arm around him. Garth shifted, his face unreadable. The wizard's eyes narrowed and then softened.

"Tell me about Bashan," Xander said.

Chip recounted the events surrounding the old Dark Elf, trying not to leave anything out. When he finished, Xander whistled. "I only encountered Bashan in the Great Battle. He was part of the Demon King's Inner Circle at the time. I heard they were childhood friends. He was a strong Blue Level who had a reputation for great cruelty. They called him the Depraved Elf, susceptible to all manner of addictions and desires. During the Elf Wars, he would torment the captured Light Elves for centuries. When released, they were almost unrecognizable. Their bodies had been mutilated in unspeakable ways, and their minds fragmented to the point where they knew not who they were. Several attacked their own families, damaged to the point of insanity.

"Bashan had no self-discipline. He gave in and satisfied any craving that appeared. He was unable to empathize with other forms of life. To him, they were objects to satisfy his selfish desires. He never knew love or kindness. His need for immediate gratification overrode all else. His only loyalty was to the Demon King, his childhood friend, but that is only because he did not want to bite the hand that fed him.

"Over the centuries, he grew bored and devised new ways of torture to give him the same feelings of pleasure. Many of the techniques and torture methods in Cave Mountain can be traced back to him. I am not surprised, when finally freed, that he abandoned his Master to focus exclusively on himself and his foul addictions.

"In the end, it looks like he finally served a purpose when he said he hated you less than his former Master. He was also a Teller. That is why the Unnamed One kept him alive. His prophecies were used to win battles and advance their cause. I suspect the Demon King was unhappy with him for not providing a correct Telling to win the Great Battle. He must have been tortured for centuries with the very techniques he created. In any event, some good may have come of his revelations."

"I do not see anything he told me as good," Chip said bitterly.

"Perhaps not now, but if it saves us, you will."

"Not if it won't save her," he said, glancing at the princess.

"I have come to terms with it," Eleanor said with a brave face, looking at each in turn. "Do not treat me any different. It is what it is. I give myself to help the world. I pray it is enough. Please be strong for me and do not waste this opportunity." Her gaze rested on Chip, who knew those last words were more for him than for anybody else. He finally nodded.

"I still don't have to like it," the boy said sullenly.

She rested her head on his shoulder. "Well, put it aside because I don't want to spend my last days with a whiner." She tickled his ribs, forcing him to laugh.

The wizard smiled. "If it were not for prophecy, I would actually know what to expect." He laughed at his own joke. "If Bashan's Telling is true, we must seek the Light Elves, specifically King Luminor. From there, we must confront the Red-Eyed King, likely before the Last Battle. We will consult any new prophecy that surfaces in the meantime."

Chip raised his hand with a perplexed look. "I am still wondering why a Dark Elf telling me she will die is different than a human telling me the same thing. Why was it so important that a human not tell me?" The wizard looked at Garth, who was not surprised by the question.

"I suggest we look at it the other way," the weapons master answered. "The human most likely to tell you such a thing would have been Xander. If he had, how would you have reacted?"

The boy pursed his lips, thinking about the scenario. "I would have been very sad. I think I would have believed him."

"How did you feel when Bashan pointed at her and told you the princess will die?" Garth asked.

"I felt a rage like no other. I vowed to do everything in my power to prevent it and not allow this despicable Dark Elf to tell me what the future holds."

The weapons master looked at him. "Those are two very different reactions which could lead to two different outcomes. We will see where this goes. That is all we can surmise for now. Regardless, do not let your guard down. No matter the prophecy, we will not easily give up the princess's life. If they want to try and take her from us, then they will pay a dear price." He clenched his hand, face hardening to a chiselled piece of granite. Chase's eyes widened. Chip felt sorry for whoever would try to take Eleanor's life in front of the weapons master, even if it was Death itself.

Xander gulped and stood up. "You have all done well today. We cannot tarry in Banfar any longer." Chip tried to protest, as they had not scanned the whole city for Dark Elves, but the wizard held up his hand. "We do not have time to go through the rest of the city. You have set the stage for others to pick up where you left off. The magic wielders who helped you yesterday will accompany the guards in your place. The one thing you need to get good at when you achieve a position of authority is to delegate. You cannot do it all, nor should you. No arguments, my boy. I also have a sixth sense for these things and believe we must leave in the morning. We have a bounty on our heads. They are coming for us. We need to get to the Wizard's Guild, where it will be safe, at least for a while. Get some rest. See you in the morning."

Chip realized he was too tired to protest and knew the wizard was right. They bade each other good night, and the three friends entered their room. He fell heavily on his cot. Chase had no choice but to clean up since black demon blood covered his clothes. He exited the room and came back a short while later. After he returned, two workers appeared, wheeling in a large wooden tub full of soapy water. Next to it, they set down two pails of warm water to wash the suds off. Eleanor told Chip she would lie with him until their Protector finished washing, and then she would order the same. Chip turned, and she leaned into him, kissing his cheek. He mumbled something, trying to form words, but he was so tired. He heard her tell Chase he had privacy because her back was towards him. Chip could not help but smile, listening to his friend splashing around the tub like a large oaf.

He felt the princess nestle her chin on his shoulder and enjoyed the warmth of her body. Then, her breathing slowed, and the boy felt a soothing darkness envelop him. He drifted off to the smell of flowers.

Chip opened his eyes to bright sunlight. He heard an infectious giggle in his ear. Bleary-eyed, he turned to see the princess staring at him amusedly.

"It's about time, sleepy head."

He groaned. "What time of day is it?"

"Mid-morning. Chase just went with Xander and Garth to get more supplies. They said not to wake you, as you need your beauty rest." The princess laughed and stood up. She was still in the same clothes from the night before. "Brush your teeth," she ordered, indicating the herbed mint mixture and soft-haired toothbrush the hotel provided for the patrons. "Hurry, I've got a surprise." She left the room with a flourish.

Chip mumbled, then got up and brushed his teeth and tongue. The mixture was potent; when he finished, he could taste fresh, clean herbs. He stretched lazily, wondering if he should wear the same clothes.

Eleanor returned with two workers who wheeled in a large tub with soapy water and two pails. They gave him and the beaming princess a funny look, then closed the door. Eleanor held up the key to the room.

"Nobody can come in now." She dropped the key on the table and started undressing. Chip blinked. She pulled her blouse over her head. He went red and started to turn away. "No, it is alright. Come join me."

He blinked a few more times.

"Uh...I...wait...uh." She laughed as he blushed. She finished undressing and stepped into the tub, letting the soapy water cover her waist. "It's fine. I will not be around forever, remember?" He gave her a sheepish look and nodded, realizing there were more important things than modesty.

"Oh, my goodness," he said, borrowing one of the wizard's phrases. He took off his dirty clothes and stood awkwardly for a moment before climbing in. She smiled happily and put her arms around his neck, drawing him to her. Before he could say a word, the princess kissed him deeply. After that, there was not much more to say. They used the time to bathe each other and cleanse themselves of all the horror they had seen, not just in the last day but in the weeks leading up to the present. The couple knew they had limited time together, so they immersed themselves in each other's embrace, dropping all pretenses and insecurities and exposing their pure, all-encompassing love for each other. They held each other for a long time, fused together in complete bliss.

A knock at the door sounded. The princess broke off their kiss, trying not to laugh.

"Who is it?" she asked, voice cracking.

"It's Chase. Are you two ready to go? Can you let me in?"

She turned to Chip, who had a big grin on his face. She flicked water at him.

"Sorry, but give me a bit more time. I am finishing bathing."

"Alright, um, I will come back in a bit," Chase said through the door. They heard him enter Xander's room.

Eleanor stood up quickly, pulling Chip with her. She lifted one of the heavy buckets filled with clean water and handed it to him. She took the other for herself and placed it on the desk beside her.

"Hurry," she said. They both climbed onto the small ledge inside the large bathtub meant for such a purpose. The water only came up to their knees. "You pour it over me first." Chip nodded, trying not to laugh, and poured the clean water over the princess while she rubbed the soap off her body. When finished, she took the empty one and set it beside the tub. She grabbed the full one off the desk and did the same for him. When finished, they both stood naked, looking at their dirty garments. "Oh, let's use magic for once to clean our clothes. We do not have time to launder them."

"But Xander said never...." Chip admonished, trying not to laugh. She put a finger to his lips.

"Once in a while is fine. He uses his magic to light his silly pipe all the time," she said, poking him in the chest. He giggled. "Hurry up, or I will."

"Oh, fine," he said, trying to break through his Wall. He forced his laughter aside, but then the idea of them standing there naked made him giggle even more, and he could not do it. She glared at him, pointing at the door, then waved her hands for him to hurry up. Her serious expression lasted a few more moments, and then his silly faces made her finally break. She laughed hysterically until they covered their mouths, desperately trying not to make loud noises.

They kept feeding off each other until they had tears in their eyes. Finally, Chip forced himself to take in big gulps of air and thought of the grotesque old Dark Elf telling him she would die. His eyes blazed red, and he lifted the clothes in the air with his Power. He passed the soiled garments through a curtain of his magic, causing the dirt to fall off somewhat.

"Good grief, you are not doing it right," she said, recovering her composure. Eleanor's eyes blazed bright brown as she took the clothes and dropped them in the bathtub water with her Power. She shook them vigorously then lifted them out. Incredibly, they came out of the water dry and clean.

Chip's eyes widened. "How did you do that?"

She laughed. "I made sure the water and dirt stayed in the tub." He looked at her funny, which made her laugh harder.

A loud knock sounded on the door, startling them. They both released the Power, and the clothes fell to the floor. "What is going on in there? I sense magic. Is everything alright?" It was Xander.

"Yes, everything is fine," the princess called out. "I dropped my... item, and it was the only way to fix it. We will be right out." They both jumped out of the tub, grabbed their clothes, and dressed hurriedly.

They heard the wizard clear his throat as if he would respond. Instead, he grunted and walked away. They gathered their things, stuffing them into the carrying bags. Chip tied the pouch with the egg to his waist, making sure it was secure. They looked around the room to ensure they had everything then stared at each other, trying not to laugh. She kissed him again and opened the door. They entered the wizard's room, pretending to look nonchalant.

Xander looked at them with mild suspicion. Garth was impassive as ever, though Chip, knowing him better than most, detected mild amusement. Chase was flopped in a chair, glowering. "It's about time."

Chip glanced around. He felt particularly good. "Let's go," he said brightly. The wizard was about to say something then thought better of it and nodded. They left the room and walked down the hall to the front desk. Patrons in the common room immediately began pointing and whispering. Captain Melvin had stationed guards at the front entrance, ready to escort them out. They dropped the keys off to the manager, who thanked them for choosing the Reindeer Inn. The party crossed the common room and entered the street.

A crowd was already waiting, and cheers erupted. "Hail the Guardian!" Chip waved, feeling even better.

Captain Melvin was waiting outside. He signalled for their horses to arrive from the stable then turned and saluted. "Good day, Mr. Guardian and Mr. Wizard, High Commander, Princess Eleanor, and Protector Chase. General Morris is waiting for you at the eastern gate."

"Thank you, Captain," Chip said, smiling. He looked at his companions momentarily in wonder, realizing that all those titles were accurate.

"Make sure you wave to the crowd again when we leave," Eleanor whispered to him. "Small things like that can have a huge impact. The key to leadership is respect. They must want to fight for you, even die for you. Showing you care is the first step."

"I always do, don't I?" Chip asked innocently.

She looked at him and smiled. "I suppose you do."

The horses arrived at the front of the inn, loaded with supplies, and they mounted. Forming a phalanx, the guards closed ranks around them and steered their way through the large crowd. The people moved out of the way, bowing and smiling. Chants of "All hail the Guardian!" followed them. Chip waved and more cheers erupted.

Captain Melvin pushed the horses into a light trot. They took several turns until the eastern wall of Banfar came into view. From there, they turned left and followed the wall to the gate. The captain explained that the route had been planned carefully. He was aware that the main street leading up to the gate from the Lower District would be packed with people trying to catch a glimpse of the Guardian. That would have impeded their approach. Even so, the crowd made it difficult to traverse the final twenty yards.

General Morris was waiting for them in front of the eastern gates. He saluted as they approached. The crowd erupted in deafening cheers. The people chanted the familiar phrase until it grew to an impressive crescendo.

Above the din, the general shouted to Chip. "I could not stop this if I tried. I will keep the gates closed after you leave for the rest of the day. I do not want a crowd harassing you all the way to your destination."

He pointed to several packhorses, which were loaded with additional supplies. "I have asked Captain Melvin to accompany you for the first leg of your journey. His men can provide an extra watch against predators and anyone who tries to follow you. Messenger pigeons arrived today, saying high-ranking soldiers from the capital would arrive within two weeks to take over Banfar's training and readiness. Other detachments will guard vital supply routes between any besieged cities and us. We will be vigilant in identifying Dark Elves who try to enter our city. We wish you good fortune, Chip Oathbinder. I look forward to fighting alongside you in the Last Battle." The boy thanked the general.

"Mr. Guardian," a voice yelled, sounding familiar. Chip looked over and saw a young soldier in a new uniform waving at him from the front of the crowd, not twenty feet away. It was Rabbit, the older boy he had met in the Lower District. He had taken Chip's advice and enlisted. The Guardian smiled and waved back. An older guard with a thick, bristling moustache suddenly appeared behind Rabbit. He said something in his ear, and the boy nodded. The man then stared at Chip and waved mechanically. Something felt off about the man, but he could not put his finger on it. Chip waved again at Rabbit then turned as the gates opened.

The enormous crowd went wild. The guards formed up, adding the new packhorses to the mix. Chip stood on his stirrups and waved to the people, feeling like he was in a dream. The noise was deafening. The phalanx turned, and the surreal landscape of the plains greeted the companions. One lone road extended straight until it disappeared into the flat horizon. Unending golden fields flanked the road on either side. The late morning sun shone upon the wheat, creating a dazzling spectacle as the stalks swayed in the wind. The noise and bustle of the crowded city seemed at complete odds with the serenity and smooth lines of the sight in front of them.

The soldiers moved forward at a measured pace. The boy turned to wave one last time at the throng before the metal gates closed. The people waved back frantically, then disappeared from view. The rhythmic chanting of the crowd accompanied them as they marched east. Eventually, the sharp wind coming off the Great Plains absorbed the sound.

It was a brisk, cold wind. Winter was coming.

Chip Oathbinder, also known as the Guardian of Humanity, sat in the middle of the phalanx, staring straight ahead, head held high. He was ready for whatever was ahead.

11

Earlier that day, a man stood before the western gates of Banfar, smiling broadly in the morning sunlight. He stroked a full beard as he scanned his surroundings.

"State your business," an older guard shouted gruffly through the small metal door near the top of the gate. He wore a clean uniform, and his tone brooked no-nonsense. The guard sported a bristling moustache.

"I am picking up supplies and looking for work."

"Where you from?" the guard asked suspiciously. "You have an accent I cannot place. Few people come to the western gates asking for work."

"I come from Vanalon. Well, a little east of it, there's a village called Forest Glen. My brother owns The Oak Inn. He headed off to Calgar while I came up this way."

The guard wrinkled his face. "Why did you not go to Calgar to fight? They would pay you."

The man showed a flash of anger but quickly smoothed it over. "I do not wish to fight. I want to find work in this city."

"Something smells fishy here. Where are your supplies?"

The man was losing his patience. "That's why I am here, you oaf."

The guard snorted. "Oaf, eh? You just bought yourself a one-way ride back where you came from."

The man looked aside for a moment, considering. "That was very foolish," he whispered.

The guard looked down again. "What did you say? I said beat it."

"Sometimes being clever can work against you, human."

"Human? Aren't we all?" the guard laughed, looking at the man as if he was daft.

The bearded man stepped forward. "No, all of us are not." His eyes suddenly blazed brightly, and an unseen force pulled the guard through the small metal door. The hole, unfortunately, was much too small, and the soldier's body snapped and twisted until it fit through. He screamed in pain, but his voice only emitted gurgling sounds as his rib cage broke and stuck in his throat. His mangled body rolled down the front of the gate to land with bones and limbs sticking out in odd directions. He shuddered once and went still.

"What in the name of the Creator?" a second guard yelled, and his face appeared in the window. As he looked out, an unseen hand lifted him into the air and tossed him backwards over the gates. The soldier landed hard on his back, which made a loud crack. He grunted and tried to raise his head but could not move. It looked like he could not feel anything below his neck.

The bearded man peered at him curiously as if studying an insect. If only he could dissect the guard. Alas, he did not have the time for such...luxuries. This soldier would never be able to see his true gifts. What a shame.

He surrounded the guard's head with the Power and twisted slowly. There was a soft crack, and the soldier went limp, eyes forever vacant. The bearded man walked over to the first guard and dipped his finger in the man's blood. The sight of it made him shiver with longing. He licked his finger clean, then shifted into the guard's form. His beard disappeared, and he tweaked his new bristling moustache.

The man then walked to the gate, lifting the inside bar with his magic, and pushed the huge metal door open enough to slip through. An old shopkeeper on the corner was staring at the gates, likely wondering why they were unmanned, but then saw the guard walk through and wave. The old man waved back and turned around, looking for a customer.

The man walked right by him into the Lower District, absently rubbing his moustache.

"Hey, Boris, where are you going?" asked the shopkeeper in amazement. "Aren't you still on duty?"

"Where is everyone?" The man, now called Boris, asked in his typical gruff voice.

The shopkeeper looked puzzled. "They are all at the eastern gate, watching the Guardian leave."

"The Guardian?" Boris asked.

"Yes, the boy wizard," the shopkeeper answered, looking at him funny.

"Ah, yes," the gatekeeper said. "I wanted to ask you about that. Let's go talk in your store."

"Sure, Boris, whatever you need." The shopkeeper opened the door and walked towards a small table at the back. "Where is your partner?" he asked over his shoulder as the guard followed him.

"That is not important right now." The voice had changed to a much higher pitch and a foreign accent. The shopkeeper spun around. Where Boris had stood was a thin man with black eyes. His skin was pure white and covered with faded scars. Skeletal hands protruded from a long black cloak.

"Who...are...you?" the shopkeeper asked in shock.

The man smiled, revealing yellow, pointed teeth. "They call me Murk."

Boris emerged a while later from the store. He had flecks of human blood on his shirt. He looked down so no one would notice his eyes as they briefly flashed, and the blood disappeared. He looked around, nodding.

Murk had learned much in a short period. The wizard boy and his companions left quite an impression on Banfar. The story of the Guardian killing an old Dark Elf who tortured humans meant Bashan was finally dead, which gave him immense pleasure. He hated the evil beast. Getting the shopkeeper to talk was easy. Murk had ways to encourage communication. He needed to find out in detail where the boy and the Orb Stealer went and what they did.

In his mind, he retraced his steps over the last few days after his Master instructed him to investigate a "disturbance." Murk reviewed the events after he slipped through the barrier to the present. He had avoided Vanalon and proceeded through the small hamlets that dotted the One Road, eventually arriving at one called Deer Run. Murk met the bearded innkeeper Ben at the White Deer Inn, where the Guardian and his companions encountered a Dark Elf in the common room. Ben did not lie to him, so he left him alive.

It was Ben's bearded form he assumed in front of the gates of Banfar. He cared not whether a human lived or died, but for the sake of conserving energy and keeping a low profile, he did not use his magic unless necessary.

His next stop was the small village of Forest Glen. The Old Oak Inn, situated at the end of town, had an innkeeper he could tell was lying. The man's wife supported her husband's lie. Demons had been killed in their barn, but they would not say by whom. He had changed to his true appearance before killing them to see the look on their faces. From there, the trail continued until he reached the fork to Fang Pass, where it was apparent they had veered off the One Road.

He could tell which horses and footprints were theirs. Murk did not need his trackers for that. When the Dark Inner Circle Elf crossed Fang Pass and gazed at his beloved Cave Mountain, he immediately knew something was wrong. The whole top of the mountain had changed. It was sunken on one side, looking like a bent old man or a worn witch's hat. The implications disturbed him.

Murk continued to follow their trail, which led into Fang Forest. He had over a dozen sinewy trackers with him and several heavily muscled demons he had added on the way. Even so, horrors were lying in wait inside the trees that even he needed to be mindful of, lest he get caught unawares. The Dark Elf did not like surprises, though he prepared for all eventualities. Murk felt tempted to skirt

Fang Forest and find out where the party had exited, but he wanted to discover what they were doing. He lost two demons to the spiders and one more to the frogs.

When he reached the clearing that housed the Dim, Murk discovered the carcasses of a Dark Elf and a dozen demons.

He rarely felt afraid unless in the presence of his Master, yet when he sent his magic into the enormous ancient tree in the middle of the clearing, he realized the Dim was gone. A cold wave of fear ran through him as Murk looked around instinctively, wondering where the spider-like creature was hiding. Then again, he was not sure the Dim ever hid. It had no need. He would have to be careful. His Master sent Zoran to Cave Mountain to feed the Dim and prepare for his arrival, but Murk did not expect it to be set free from the tree so soon. Then a thought dawned on him. Zoran was also instructed to use the Dim to attack the boy wizard. It made sense for him to unleash it if the boy was here. Then why the great release of magic? Could they have destroyed the mountain in their fight with the creature? That would be impossible for anyone but his Master. The amount of Power necessary would be almost unimaginable.

He set his thoughts and conjectures aside and continued following the trail. He noticed the party had allied themselves with another small group of humans. The tracks indicated two men, a woman, and two small children. He paused, looking at the clearing one last time. The humans that joined them would likely have been sacrificed to the Dim. The boy wizard had intervened to save them. Being young, he probably had an idealistic view of good and evil and was willing to do anything to help a few measly humans. Murk laughed inwardly at the foolishness of youth.

The two groups must have joined forces and walked to the forest's edge. From there, the humans they saved took the horses and rode back towards the pass. The boy wizard and his four companions had continued on foot, following the forest's edge, before exiting on the northeastern side. They then traversed rocky ground, which was much more difficult to track. He signalled for his Tracker demons to take over. They dropped on all fours, picking up and following the scent. They were created specifically for this. The trail led to the steep slope on the northern side of Cave Mountain. He surmised their goal was to approach from the side Zoran would least expect and surprise the Inner Circle Dark Elf.

When Murk crested the top of the slope, he was greeted by a plethora of demon bodies. They littered the entrances to the caves. He searched the first cave on the left and found several piles of ash. The Dark Elf knew instantly that the Dim had touched them. He could also see scratch marks on the stone from the creature's metallic claws. Another stab of fear went through him.

Where was the beast? He knew it could not die, so it must be somewhere. He searched the back of the cave and found the ceiling collapsed around the corner. Could the Dim be under the pile of rocks? His eyes blazed as he sent his magic out to penetrate the stone. There were no bodies. He concluded that the boy wizard must have dropped the ceiling to slow the Dim. It had not worked.

Murk looked around, realizing this was where the villagers were kept as prisoners. An array of human belongings peeked out of the crushed stone. He retraced his steps and checked the cave on the far right. It contained Dark Elf belongings, several more demon bodies and piles of ash. This was where Zoran had made his base. Murk was most interested in the center tunnel, the entrance into Cave Mountain.

If the Dim was still in the vicinity, it would likely be in there. He also expected to find the dead wizard boy and his companions. It was improbable they had escaped the creature—unless they had dropped the mountain on it, which was nigh impossible. They had likely tried to fight the beast with magic, and the mountain had crushed them all. Even that was farfetched but not impossible. It would be much easier to collapse a mountain from the inside.

Murk entered the main cave entrance, sending his trackers ahead. If the Dim was lurking about, his demon companions would die first, giving him a chance to flee. His life was worth theirs and much more. He was, after all, Inner Circle. Moreover, he had a talent that made him much more dangerous than all of them: he was a shapeshifter.

Murk continued walking down the central tunnel and found a dead Dark Elf with a crushed head and then a single pile of ash in front of it. Could it be? He sent his magic into the ash and faintly sensed an old presence, a familiarity. It was Zoran. Real fear washed over him at that moment. The Dim had touched Zoran. Murk's mind reeled. The creature, for whatever reason, was not following orders anymore. They could not control it, not even his Master. He looked around hurriedly, trembling. He had assumed that if he found the Dim, Zoran would be close enough to reign it in. Zoran was now dead.

Murk had no choice but to press forward. His Master wanted a report on the disturbance. So far, the report was such that he did not want to be anywhere within the Demon King's vicinity when told the news. His Master's rage would be unfathomable.

Moving forward, Murk and the trackers found the solid gold entrance doors. The seal was broken. The one on the right was ripped off its hinges and had a deep hollow in the middle from repeated strikes. The Dark Elf's eyes widened. It appeared the Guardian had entered his Master's lair and shut the door on the Dim. Evidently, that only held it for so long.

The implications of this were getting more sinister. He knew the Demon King had sealed the entrance with his Power. No one should be able to break the seal and enter his home. Was the boy wizard that capable? He shook his head and stepped through, sending the demons in first with a ball of light to illuminate the way.

Soon after, they reached the large foyer with silver doors. A significant hollow dent was in the middle of one of them, but they remained closed. He looked at the ground. The boy and his companions had entered the throne room and locked the doors which held. Faint scratch marks on the stone went left down another tunnel. The Dim had decided to find another way to get at them. The trackers indicated they could not smell the creature. It was scentless. However, he could track it easily by the scratch marks on the stone. The Dim had no need for stealth.

The Dark Elf faced the silver doors. Using magic, he lifted the inside bar, set it aside, and lightly pushed the door to the right. The throne room was empty. He sent in his ball of light, illuminating the diamond throne. The sight of it brought forth ancient memories of grandeur.

He remembered sitting at the long table heaped with all manner of food. Demons lined the walls, torturing countless human slaves. The Inner Circle had sat at that table, gorging on a vast assortment of food and drink brought in by trembling humans. Off to the sides and back, Dark Elves of higher ranks satisfied their whims and desires, however repugnant to others. Nothing was off limits.

Some of the Inner Circle, including him, had even developed a taste for human flesh. They would chew on the soft meat of a human rib bone and then wash it down with warmed blood. Slashar, a brutish Inner Circle Dark Elf, loved the eyeballs. Murk preferred the organs, finding the muscles too chewy.

The Demon King found it amusing and encouraged such experimentation. Certain haughty Inner Circle members frowned on the practice, believing humans should only be food for demons, not Dark Elves. Murk knew it was an acquired taste, and they only needed to give it a chance.

The worst was Bashan. He was a slave to every addiction imaginable. Whereas Murk usually tortured for a purpose, with an appropriate modicum of pleasure, Bashan did it for pure joy. He would create methods of pain and suffering that pushed the envelope of depravity. The Master allowed it until they had their disagreement. Bashan had paid for his insolence, daring to blame his Master for not releasing the Dim earlier in the Last Battle. He suffered for centuries. It served him right, Murk thought. He had no love for humans, but the things Bashan did were...disagreeable, even to one such as him.

Murk had been in charge of the assassins, which invariably involved a high level of skill in torture. He had gleaned important information countless times due to his efficient techniques. His unique shapeshifting ability was the perfect complement to his craft. During the Elf Wars, he had assassinated many Light Elves. He tortured some to gather information regarding the war and then dispatched them with indifference. He had even made an assassination attempt on King Luminor.

Murk had worked his way up the Light Elf ranks for years, concealing his identity. The king was well protected, so when an opportunity finally arose, he struck a tad prematurely, only injuring Luminor instead of killing him. He chalked it up to youthful exuberance. He sighed, realizing how King Luminor's death would have changed history.

He had been so close. After the attempt, Murk barely escaped with his life. He then had to face his Master, who was not pleased with his failure.

The Dark Elf touched the numerous scars over his body. The Master had given him to Bashan to be tortured for a decade. He was not permitted to heal his scars. By his Master's orders, he would wear them forever as a reminder of his failure to assassinate Luminor.

He shook himself from his reverie and proceeded through the throne room. It was then that he noticed the massive cracks in the walls. The mountain's collapse on the eastern side had affected the structural integrity of the tunnels, even the throne room.

The Dark Elf passed the diamond throne and exited the back of the room, listening for any sounds. Dead silence greeted him. The trackers followed the scent of the boy wizard and his companions through the Demon King's bedroom suite. Several rare artifacts had fallen and broken from whatever shook the mountain. The priceless value of the items meant nothing to him. He had no use for such things.

Murk continued through the council room and down long tunnels that sloped through the Dark Elf quarters to the demon chambers. Spider web cracks ran along most tunnels and intensified as he went deeper. Pieces of rock littered the ground, and whole rooms had collapsed. The tunnel finally ended where the stairs should have gone down to the center of the mountain, but they were completely gone. The entrance had caved in, buried by an unimaginable amount of stone.

A sharp stab of fear entered his heart when he realized what was under all that rock. The eggs were his Master's most prized possessions, more valuable than all the diamonds in the world. Only the Inner Circle knew of their existence. Nobody else was permitted through the door leading to the stairs. It would not surprise him if the boy wizard's body were under it all, along with his companions. The Dim had likely trapped them on the island in the lake, and in a last-ditch effort to save themselves, they brought the mountain down. It was now a tomb.

He closed his eyes and sent his magic out, expecting to find bodies. The Dark Elf reached deep into the mounds of rock and unexpectedly felt a strong life form. It was a dragon, but which one? He tried to communicate with the being but received only one image, which was crystal clear. It thought of him as a lesser elf and would only communicate with the Demon King. That at least gave him his answer. It was the black egg.

He searched longer, looking for the remnants of the white egg or other bodies, but could not locate anything. The black egg completely shut itself off him, raging that he would have the nerve to communicate with it. He laughed out loud. Did the dragon not understand that he could shapeshift into anything he wanted as long as he touched it? Since he had ridden dragons during the Elf Wars, he could turn into one. The only limitation would be the magical aspect. He would have all the physical attributes of a dragon, which were formidable, but not its magic, only his own.

In any event, he preferred the attributes of other demons his Master had created over the millennia. He would not dwell on the snobbery of a dragon. He had more important things to do. His Master would be furious that the white egg was missing, but at least the black one had survived. He shuddered at the thought of how much Power it would take to unbury the egg. Only his Master possessed that kind of strength.

Murk had no choice but to retrace his steps, returning to the front entrance. He hiked around the mountain's base to the eastern side. He sent his trackers out ahead to see if there were any trails. He guessed that the wizard boy and his companions were buried there.

That was where the Dim likely caught up to them. He would identify the bodies and then report back to his Master. He was not looking forward to providing the Demon King with ill tidings. There was always a chance he would not survive it, regardless of who was to blame.

Suddenly, he heard loud shrieks and mewls. The trackers had found something. He transformed into one of them, running as they did, with long, lithe muscles. Their bodies were honed for speed, and he ate the ground up, arriving at their location. Murk returned to his true Dark Elf form and examined what they pointed at on the ground. Incredibly, it was the boy wizard's tracks and all his companions. They had survived.

His shock was difficult to control. He turned to study the mountain, amazed at how much its shape had changed. The center had completely sunk in on itself, with the east side jutting out then down. He raised his arms and sent his magic deep into the ground. He was looking for the possible life form of the other egg, or anything else for that matter. He took his time, sensing each piece.

He was about to give up when he went over a spot where not much was there—nothing, in fact. He went back and hovered over it, then felt another jolt of fear as he felt the spot slightly alter. It was as if something was in there changing its shape. With cold certainty, he knew it was the Dim. It was scratching the stone, trying to get out.

The implications staggered him. That would mean the boy and his companions had collapsed the side of the mountain on the creature, trapping it. Even if he was linked with the Orb Stealer, Xandrostika, the boy could not accomplish such a thing. A chilling thought entered his mind. What about the white dragon? If he had the egg, could it have helped him? Was it even capable of that? Too many questions without answers. He needed more information.

Murk looked at the tracks on the ground. They were only a few days old. He decided it was time to speed things up. He transformed back into a tracker. They were built for speed, and he enjoyed the freedom of the form. The muscled demons accompanying them were much slower. They would fall behind and catch up while the others rested. He cared not whether they died from lack of sleep or exhaustion. If they survived, he would put them to use. Otherwise, they were expendable.

Murk travelled at speed for the rest of the day, reaching the Great Plains by nightfall. He chided himself for not stopping to torture someone earlier about the new geography of the land. He should have learned more about the cities and local news. After all, it had been three millennia since he was here. He did not like the openness of the plains, so he slept in a copse of trees at the edge of the foothills.

In the morning, he awoke refreshed. His movement awakened the trackers, who sprang to their feet, ready to continue. Their sole purpose was to track prey and then rend flesh from bone. He would have to feed them soon to maintain their energy. He could see they were getting restless. He transformed again, and they all sprinted off at a frightening pace. The demon trackers led him straight east across the endless wheat fields.

On the way, Murk spied prairie wolves and, surprisingly, a huge mountain wolf. It was cunning and disappeared when he caught a glimpse. By midmorning, they had arrived near the gates of a small unknown city, which must have sprung up after the barrier. The wizard boy could still be here as the tracks were only a couple of days old. They had made up good time. He instructed the demons to wait for him outside the city. He told the trackers to feast at will on the prairie dogs while he was gone, but not the mountain wolf. They were unlikely to catch it anyway, and he did not want to lose any in an unnecessary fight. The Dark Elf then transformed into Ben from the White Deer Inn and approached the gates.

Murk now knew the city was called Banfar. As the gate guard Boris, he replayed the events in his head, making sure not to miss anything. He liked to be thorough, putting the pieces in place. Much of his pleasure came from the chase and devising an appropriate assassination plan, which required information. The more, the better.

Boris absently stroked his bristling moustache. The Dark Elf turned left from the shopkeeper's store and walked the almost empty streets of the Lower District. Food would have to wait. He walked across town and spied the huge crowd awaiting the so-called Guardian. It was late morning. The shopkeeper was right about the people obsessing over this wizard boy. Murk decided to keep his current form. Being Boris allowed him to push through the crowd without incident. When the people saw he was a guard, they did not protest. He spied a line of horses approaching the gate from the right, recognizing the orb stealing wizard, who was now an old man. He had not seen Xandrostika in a very long time. He pushed his way through the noisy humans.

The horses had stopped before the gates. Murk was right near the front of the crowd when an older boy in a guard uniform yelled "Mr. Guardian" at the wizard boy. They both waved at each other. Boris then put his hand on the young man's shoulder, asking him if he knew the Guardian personally, and he nodded.

Boris looked up, noticing the boy wizard staring at him. He was an expert at reading people's expressions over the millennia and knew the so-called Guardian found him odd. The boy's instincts were telling him what he saw was wrong. Boris was really a Dark Elf. Murk waved at the Guardian, who finally waved back, still unsure what was bothering him. The elf was impressed at his intuition.

The eastern gates of Banfar opened, and the party began to move out. Murk noticed the Guardian rode with the Orb Stealer, two Protectors, and a girl. A dozen guards surrounded them. He saw the boy and girl smile at each other as the gates opened. The Dark Elf knew instantly they were in love. The thought of that emotion made his bile rise. Nevertheless, a thrill went through Murk that he could take something so precious away from the boy before capturing him. His Master would be pleased.

The Guardian waved once more to the crowd and then rode east into the plains. The gates closed behind them. Murk looked at the young man beside him, wondering if it was worth his time to torture the boy for more information.

He decided to be blunt. "How do you know the Guardian?" he asked.

"Oh, I met him in the Lower District. He told me to enlist to fight against the demons. You are Boris, right? I'm Rabbit." He held out his human hand.

Murk thought about killing him right there, if only to give the Guardian more pain, but then realized that Rabbit barely knew the boy wizard. He shrugged and shook his hand.

"Hey, Boris, shouldn't you be at the gates?"

Murk looked to the right to see who was asking him the question. It appeared to be a captain, judging by the man's uniform. Without responding, the Dark Elf turned and moved through the crowd, pushing into the throng. He looked back once to see Rabbit standing slack-jawed. He heard a commotion behind him and gained another few steps before ducking down and shapeshifting, then reappearing. He felt a hand on his shoulder.

"Is that you, Boris?" It was a soldier who had been standing near the captain.

"No, I'm Rabbit, sir." Murk smiled lopsidedly as the young man had.

"Oh, I thought you were Boris." The guard looked confused. "I thought you were back there?"

Murk thought on the fly. He needed to get out of the situation without making a disturbance. "Yes, I move fast." He grinned. "That's why they call me Rabbit. Boris went that way." He pointed ahead of him.

The guard, still looking bewildered, nodded and pushed past him. Murk turned and bent to tie his shoe. When he rose, he had the face of the shopkeeper. The real Rabbit walked by with more guards, apparently all looking for Boris. The boy looked at him, blinked once, and continued scanning the crowd. The shopkeeper moved away from them and exited on the crowd's other side. He did not like this form, as the shopkeeper was old.

Murk put his hand on the neck of a large, muscled man, yelling, "All hail the Guardian." The man glared at him at first, then smiled when he realized it was an old shopkeeper who was excited for the moment. The man patted him on the shoulder and walked away.

Moments later, Murk bent down to scratch his knee and stood up. He was now large and heavily muscled.

The Dark Inner Circle Elf decided to spend the rest of the day inquiring about the Guardian and his activities in the city. The more he knew about the boy and his companions, the more information he would use to set his trap. He would reunite with his trackers in the morning, sending one of them back to his Master with a note to report his discoveries. The bad news regarding the collapsed mountain, the missing white egg, and the trapped Dim would enrage his Master to the point where many in his immediate vicinity would die. The Dark Elf was happy he was not the one relaying the news.

Murk was already calculating what form he would take to attack them on the Great Plains. His Master had created demons the likes of which humanity had never seen. On Demon Island, Murk had made sure to touch each of the beautifully designed creatures so he could assume their shape when desired. The Dark Elves had three millennia to perfect their killing machines. He could turn into any one of them.

Besides his Master, Murk knew he was more dangerous than anyone in the world. He was a shapeshifter. There was nobody like him.

12
———

The cool air of the Great Plains felt invigorating. The openness was a welcome relief after the confines of the busy, crowded city. Chip bathed in the late afternoon sun, closing his eyes occasionally to listen to the wind.

They had ridden all day at a brisk pace through the endless wheat fields. They passed some travellers going to Banfar. Many were job seekers or outcasts looking for a place that would take them. Every so often, they would see a farmer's homestead with dogs running around the yard and smoke rising from the chimney.

Field hands dotted the landscape, tending and harvesting the crops. It was autumn, the busiest time of year for farmers. They could see the occasional small lake or pond in the distance, the afternoon sun sparkling off the water.

"There's a farmer I know up the road who may let us borrow his barn for the night," Captain Melvin called from the front of the phalanx. "Would that be acceptable, Mr. Guardian?" The boy was still unused to the name.

"Call me Chip," he said, "And yes, that would be more than fine."

"I'm sorry, sir. It is protocol to use the title. I would be more comfortable saying Guardian if you would be kind enough to let me," he said pleadingly.

"Very well, Captain. I do not pretend to be high and mighty. I am only an orphan."

"You are much more than an orphan, Mr. Guardian," he answered. "Much more."

A short while later, Melvin turned down a farmer's driveway on the right. A quaint house and barn grew more prominent as they approached. Cows grazed behind the home in the distance. A man stepped out onto the porch, holding a tobacco pipe. He had black hair with grey at the temples. Two older children followed the man out, peering around him to see who the newcomers were.

"Greetings, Ulrich. How are things?" asked Captain Melvin, dismounting and shaking his hand.

"Good as can be expected, I suppose. Lots of work to do." He looked at the rest of the party. "These must be important people to have such an escort. To what do I owe the honour?" the farmer asked. The door opened, and a woman with an apron joined him. The children stayed on the porch.

"Ulrich and his wife Anna, I present to you the Guardian of Humanity, the Grand Wizard Xander, Princess Eleanor of Vanalon, and Protectors Garth Stone and Chase Longfellow." The farmer's mouth dropped open, and his wife's eyes widened.

"Good grief, Captain Melvin. Do you wish to give me a heart attack?" Ulrich feigned, clutching his chest. "I don't know what all that means, but it sounds mighty important. My house is yours."

The captain chuckled. "Your house is not necessary, Ulrich. We would, however, ask kindly for the use of your barn to bed for the night. If not, we understand."

"Oh heavens, trading the barn for the house is a steal in my books. It is yours as long as you wish. Up until the harvest in two weeks, that is. Then I need it." Ulrich looked at the others. "I assume you are all hungry. My wife Anna here would love for you to try her roast lamb. It has been cooking over a spit since lunchtime. No one makes better."

"Oh yes, that sounds delicious," Chase gushed before anyone could answer.

Anna took over. "Ulrich, take these guests to the barn. I will prepare a fabulous meal befitting their station. Run along now. It will be dark soon."

Captain Melvin laughed. "I was going to say we carry our own food rations, but I know you would insist. Very well, that is kind."

"Kind indeed," said Xander. "Without farmers, the rest of us would be nothing." Anna nodded and winked at him.

Ulrich showed them to the barn, pushing farming implements aside to make room for everyone. There was a large metal stove with a huge stack of firewood beside it. The farmer gathered the starter material and a short while later, had an intense blaze going.

"This will ward off the evening chill," he said, looking at Melvin. "Dinner should be ready shortly." The captain thanked him as Ulrich showed himself out.

Chase stretched. "I'm famished." He rubbed his belly.

"You are always famished," the wizard said shortly. He looked at the captain. "How long to the next village?"

"Two day's ride to Moose Pond. Between, we will camp on the plains."

The wizard nodded. "Let's find out from the farmer if there have been any strange tidings."

"Yes, Mr. Wizard."

True to her word, the farmer's wife, Anna, returned after a short period with heaping platters of roast lamb, corn, mashed potatoes, and fresh bread. Her children, a boy and a girl, helped carry in the dishes. The men dug in heartily, sharing stories of Banfar, one more preposterous than the next. The whole room was full of friends telling stories, drinking ale, and eating wholesome food. The warm fire kept the chill out of the autumn evening. The companions sat across each other on wooden benches, elbows resting on the rough-hewn oak tables. Chip looked around, wishing he could stay for a week.

Chase was holding his second glass of ale, telling three guards about the battle of Vanalon. Xander talked low with Captain Melvin, who listened with attentive ears. The weapons master was surrounded by several young recruits, showing them a sword technique.

A barn cat with orange stripes wandered in. It inspected the room imperiously, likely wondering who dared enter its territory. The animal traversed the room, pausing to sniff here and there. Its eyes met Chip's, and he felt a flash of menace. The boy thought he would not want to be a mouse in this cat's barn. He looked again, but the cat had moved on. He squeezed Eleanor's hand.

"You like it here, do you not?" she said, looking into his green eyes.

"Yes. It reminds me of… I guess the stable in Vanalon. It feels like home, in a way. Good food, honest people, hard work, and fresh air. Yes, I like it."

Eleanor looked around. "I know what you mean. In a way, I have been spoiled in the palace." He expressed a mock look of shock. She swatted him. "My mother tried to surround me with normal things as much as possible. I like this place too. There is no pretentiousness here. People say what they mean." She looked around and laughed. "You would not like the high court in Toron. The nobility is insufferable. High King Dominor seems somewhat reasonable, but the princes and the various dukes and duchesses are spoiled."

He looked at her. "I don't understand why, with so much wealth and power, they need to act that way. Do they not like helping others?"

"Many feel they are better than others. They feel entitled and deserve their station in life. They have never worn a commoner's shoes."

Chip shook his head. "They should be forced to, if only for a week. It will make them grateful for what they have and teach them to treat others with respect. This farmer understands, and he's wealthy."

The princess laughed. "This farmer is a commoner to them. He is not educated, travelled or discerning." The boy glared at her. She put her hand over his. "I am simply saying that they do not consider him wealthy."

"To me, this farmer is very rich. He has much land, good food, a nice family, and is kind. What more do you want?" Chip looked at her, turning his palms up.

She cupped his cheek. "You are so precious. If only the nobility could see like you do." She smiled at his puzzled expression. He did not understand rich people.

The farmer came in with his wife, asking after everyone. Anna noticed the cat and shook her finger at him. "How did you get in here, you stinker? I thought you were in your cathouse out back." She picked him up and threw the feline out the door. He managed to scratch her before he flew through the air. "Ouch. I will get you for that. That's not like you!" She raised her fist at him then hurried back, rubbing her arm. She looked at Ulrich. "He never does that."

The farmer shrugged. "He's getting old, dear. Like us."

Xander cleared his throat. "Ulrich, I was wondering if you had any tidings?"

He looked at the wizard. "Tidings, sir?"

"Yes, anything... strange."

Ulrich folded his arms. "Hmm. Come to think of it, yes. Last night, a farmer who resides just north of Banfar passed through here in his wagon, complaining that his cow had been eaten by what appeared to be a mountain wolf." The wizard feigned surprise. "A creature was also found a day ago west of Banfar, killed by a brown tiger. It was naked and grey, with black eyes and blood. Scary-looking thing. Also, strange men have walked the road with black-hooded cloaks."

Xander nodded. "They are Dark Elf scouts. The tales are true, I am afraid. Vanalon has defeated one demon army, but it will be overwhelmed soon. When the barrier falls, the Demon King will push east with his army, take Calgar, and advance on Toron. This farm is further north, so you should be spared, at least for a while. You wheat farmers will be critical to supplying our armies. Officials will talk to everyone shortly, coordinate grain shipments, and find ways to protect you. Keep your ears open to news from Banfar. If it falls, you need to take your family to safety."

Ulrich and Anna gave each other worried looks. The farmer sighed. "So, it's true then. That is what I feared. We will help in any way we can." He put his arm around Anna, who trembled.

The wizard spoke with compassion. "Keep to your business. Avoid anyone who does not show their face. Dark Elves are wandering the land, gathering information. Demons sometimes accompany them. They are still in hiding, so they should not threaten you openly. There is ample game grazing on the plains to satisfy their hunger. Your hospitality is much appreciated."

The wizard flipped him a gold coin.

The farmer's eyes widened. "We do not require payment. It is our pleasure." Ulrich tried to hand back the coin.

"It is not negotiable. Keep it. The demons will push many people east. Use it to help them if you wish. In the meantime, perhaps one more glass of ale if you can spare it." Xander smiled.

Ulrich nodded with a laugh. "As many as you like." The farmer hurried off with his wife.

The party enjoyed pumpkin pie with fresh whipped cream for dessert, and afterwards, the children came in and played tunes on their violins. Some of the men danced, mainly for the amusement of others. The ale passed a little too freely, but all enjoyed boisterous stories and good cheer. Chip could relax for the first time in many weeks and even stood up to dance with the princess for a song.

He wished the night would never end. The barn cat wandered in again, watching them balefully in their revelry. It walked over and sat next to the princess. She was laughing at Chase, who was pretending to dance like Miss Owl. She reached down to scratch it behind the ears. Its claws came out for a moment, but then it scurried away, hackles raised. She shrugged and started laughing again at the young Protector. The evening finally ended when the captain ordered everyone to bed, worried they might stay up the whole night for all the fun they were having.

The soldiers performed watch duty. Xander offered to take turns, but the captain insisted. Chip noticed the cat staring at him strangely, making him shiver for some reason, but it left before Melvin could usher it out. Xander locked the barn door, glancing outside as if finding something odd, then shrugged and resumed his seat. Nothing eventful happened the rest of the night.

The men woke at first light, some holding their heads. With a party that large, it was difficult to sleep longer. The farmer and his family brought heaping plates of sizzling bacon, farm-fresh eggs, fried potatoes, and warm bread. They ate to contentment, some less than others, and were mounted and ready to go shortly thereafter.

Chip looked at the farm with a wistful expression. He wished they could stay longer. The boy watched the farmer's daughter approach the barn cat, who peered at them malevolently.

"Oh, Oliver, why the mean face?" She tried to pick him up, but he slashed her viciously and hissed, then ran off behind the house. The girl started crying.

"Leave him be," her mother said. "I don't know what's gotten into him."

"May fortune and the Creator shine on your travels," Ulrich said, standing to the side. They bid him well and rode off. The family waved until they were out of sight.

Murk regained his form as he walked behind the farmhouse. Bits of blood coated his finger from the girl's arm. He tasted it and paused for a long moment. He desperately wanted to go back and kill the entire family. Even as the enjoyable thought entered his head, the Dark Elf knew it was too risky. He needed to conserve his energy for the coming ambush and could not jeopardize his element of surprise by alerting them to his presence. He walked past the shed at the back of the farmhouse, glancing at the decapitated body of the real barn cat lying in the wheat. He had gleaned much information over the night. Murk felt disappointed for almost losing control when he sat near the princess.

In the barn cat's feral state, it was easier to kill on a whim. He could have ended her life right then, but escape would have been challenging. Still, he had almost given in. The Dark Elf scolded himself to be patient. It had been a long time since he practiced his craft, and he needed to take it slowly. He licked the remaining blood off his finger, then turned into a demon tracker, and bounded off through the fields.

Captain Melvin maintained a good speed all morning, stopping only for a light lunch. By mid-afternoon, most men had shaken off their hangover and resumed their good humour. As evening approached, they decided to camp near a pond off the road. Tents were set up with the soldiers clustered to one side. They reheated leftover lamb stew in a large pot resting on hot coals. The smell of rosemary permeated the air. After dinner and small talk, the group retired early, with the soldiers taking the first watch, two at a time.

It was deep in the night when a mournful howl broke the silence, causing Chip to leap out of his tent with eyes blazing a ferocious red. The wizard also sprang out, hands raised. The men on watch thought they saw something at the firelight's edge. They searched the camp's perimeter and found demon footprints. It looked like at least a dozen demons had encircled the camp. Two large, wicked-looking three-toed footprints were found behind the princess's tent, causing her to go white. Afterwards, Chip had Eleanor sleep with him and Chase. He was taking no chances. Watches increased to three people. No further events transpired that evening.

In the morning, Captain Melvin looked concerned. Most footprints were made by long, slender feet with small talons, likely built for running. They were demonic.

"They are trackers," Xander said. "The Demon King sent them to follow and kill us." He looked at Chip. "Or capture us."

The boy looked up. "Why don't we find them?" he asked coldly.

"They are built for speed and can easily outrun horses, maintaining a full run for days. It's a fool's errand," answered the wizard.

"What was that three-toed print?" the boy asked. "Does it look familiar?"

The wizard's face took on a somber look. "The three toes, as you know, signify the assassin demon, but this could be anything. I have never seen one this large. The Demon King makes all manner of creatures bred for different purposes. He could have made a much larger assassin. It will be cunning and very fast. My concern is that the footprints were found behind her tent..." He left the thought unfinished.

"We will be vigilant," Chip said, eyes smouldering.

"The captain can only guide us for a few days, remember?" Xander reminded him.

"On the contrary," Captain Melvin interjected, "my men and I took an oath to protect humanity in the presence of Chip Oathbinder. What better way than to defend the Guardian himself? We want to accompany you to your final destination." He looked at the rest of the soldiers, who nodded wholeheartedly.

Xander acknowledged them gravely. "Very well. Your help is much appreciated. Let us be on our way but keep alert."

They rode faster, reaching the town of Moose Pond by late afternoon. It was more of a small village with homes clustered along the southern end of Moose Lake. Apparently, on the far side, its namesake wandered the marshes. The moose were quite docile unless someone strayed near their young.

The group of travellers ended up taking over the lone inn for the night. A few other patrons were grandfathered in, but Xander bought up all the remaining rooms for safety reasons. He asked that the inn remain closed to the rest of the public for the evening. Seeing the gold coins, the innkeeper, a stout fellow wearing a black apron, agreed immediately. They received a whole pot of moose stew and an endless supply of fresh bread. Ale was on the house.

Knowing the stakes had been raised, the men abstained from imbibing more than one mug with their meal. For the remainder of the trip, they would stay alert. Being hunted by a pack of demons would likely scare anyone sober. They made small talk in low voices for the rest of the evening. By night's end, the fire had been banked, and the pot of stew sat empty. The innkeeper bade them good night. Watches were still set, but nothing eventful occurred.

The companions travelled east over the next several days, sleeping on the open plains as there were no villages. On the fifth day, two soldiers were found dead in their tents, throats slashed. There were no footprints. Nobody could figure out how the murderer got in. The next day, they arrived at another village and rented out the rest of the inn. In the morning, blood leaked out of one of the rooms. Two more guards were dead, throats slashed. Worse, the men's chests had been ripped open and their hearts eaten.

"The guards are getting nervous," Captain Melvin whispered to Xander in the common room. "The men on watch saw and heard nothing."

"We understand if you want to leave," the wizard said.

"Leave? If anything, we have no choice but to stay since the danger has increased, and stay we will. Do you have any idea how this is happening?"

"No, Captain. All I can say is whatever wants to eat a human's heart is almost certainly a demon or Dark Elf. No other animal or race I know of would kill in this way."

The captain leaned in. "How much further to the Guild?"

"Three days," the wizard answered. "There is only one more town between here and the fortress. It is Thundar, a day's ride from this village. After that, the road turns sharply south to Toron, where we leave it to head east. The Wizard's Guild is somewhat isolated on purpose. Most people do not seek the Guild coming from the direction of Banfar. From Toron, there is an actual road going north, but we are far west of that. To our right is Lake Supper, the largest lake on the Great Plains. Following its shore will lead us into Thundar by nightfall.

The captain nodded. "We are down to eight soldiers. Our lives are yours. We will see this to the end."

"You are a good man, Captain," Xander said. Melvin saluted and stood up to prepare for their departure.

They continued trekking across the seemingly endless plains and arrived in Thundar before dusk. The air had turned noticeably cooler as the autumn progressed. To the east, they finally saw a smudge of low foothills. On the right, Lake Supper extended as far as the eye could see. They entered the town with the sun low on their backs. This town was much larger than the villages they had passed crossing the Great Plains. The people, however, seemed an unfriendly lot. Necklaces and pendants were hung above storefronts, and strange symbols were painted on the doors of houses. The people gave them suspicious glares and hurried about their business. Chip watched as an old man made a warding gesture as they passed.

The wizard noticed the boy's surprise. "These are superstitious folk. Everything here is about signs and omens. It is a fishing village. The catch depends on supply, overfishing, wind, rain, tides, time of day, and so on. To them, each sign is an omen. Successful fishermen and women can read the signs. They attribute nothing to luck. They are receptive to prophecy in all its forms. Thundar has the highest concentration of Seers and Tellers in Amrika. The residents and travellers listen to them, paying good money to hear their fortunes. Some tell when and where to fish or what their future holds. Charlatans abound in all things where money is involved, but true Seers can still be found."

They continued through the village. "What is that?" Chip asked. Up ahead, with its back to the lake, a tall house stood alone, set back from the road. It was painted entirely black. Various rock structures covered the expansive lawn in intricate formations. He could see an old woman wearing a black dress sitting in a large rocking chair on the porch. Pendants and charms hung from the top of the verandah, running along the whole front of the house. She stared straight ahead, rocking slowly. Even from this distance, he could see her eyes were pure white.

"That is Zinduk, a magic wielder," Xander said. "She is considered by many to be the most powerful Seer in Thundar. She does not take appointments anymore. She will stay quiet for years, then utter a pronouncement. This particular Teller will only approach you. If you step on her property uninvited, she will throw a yellow fireball at you. Not even the Thundar guards will trespass."

He glanced at the weapons master beside him, and they shared a look.

A scream suddenly sounded. The old woman rocking in her chair stopped moving. The Seer stood up with unnatural movements, trying to straighten her bent body, which had a pronounced hump. Her white eyes looked at the sky as she screamed again, and then she looked straight at Chip. The old woman slowly raised her arm and pointed at him. He felt a chill pass through his body. Xander raised his hand, and Captain Melvin stopped the procession.

Keeping her gaze locked on his, the old woman stepped down from the porch and began scuttling towards him like a spider. He could not believe how fast she could move. The Seer stopped at the edge of the property, scanning them all then settling her gaze once more on the boy. Her hair stood out in violent disarray. Chip realized a white milky film covered what appeared to be yellow eyes. Her face was craggy and worn as if ravaged by too many visions.

"Greetings, Zinduk," the wizard said politely.

"Quiet, old man," she said hoarsely, exposing several brown teeth. "You have evaded death long enough. You have a scant chance of avoiding what is coming, Orb Stealer. Even your Protector cannot save you. The boy Seer was right." She turned to the princess, and her craggy face softened. "You will die first, dear. The boy loves you. Your death will make him mad with rage and grief. He will walk a path turned upside down. If he falls to either side, all is lost. It is love though that will make it possible."

She turned to Chip. "You were never supposed to be born. The Balance created you when the laws bent." She leaned forward, white spittle flecking her lips. "You can save us, boy, but only if your love is strong enough. The Paths...are disappearing. The Nothing is eating them. If you tarry too long, there will be none left. The red-eyed one waits for you. He is not who you think. The truth may break the world, Guardian."

Chip blinked in surprise. She laughed, cackling shrilly. "It is just one of your names. The King of the Elves provides a sliver of hope if you can find him." She stepped back, shaking her head. "The prophecies are fragmenting, unravelling. Too much free choice is dangerous. If the Balance breaks, then Chaos will reign forever. Only a thread holds the Dark Lord back. He is coming...." She stopped in mid-sentence then leapt back and hissed. "What is this?" She looked around quickly, settling her eyes on a young guard at the back of the procession. "A great evil rides with you. I cannot see it, but it is here." She scuttled backwards. "I have spoken my part. The boy Seer will reveal the rest. My time is over."

She grunted, coughing hoarsely, then moved backwards to the porch, making warding gestures at them.

"Well, that was awkward," Chase said to no one in particular. Xander stared at the young soldier in the back. His name was Tom.

"Why did she look at me?" Tom asked with genuine surprise. His horse shifted, its tail trying to swat a fly off its rump, which flew away. Xander's eyes blazed blue as he sent out his magic to envelope the man and horse. After a moment, he withdrew his presence. Nothing seemed amiss. He heard the old witch cackle again behind him.

"Evil is following us. There is no question," the wizard said, ignoring her. "Zinduk likely senses its taint on us. We will be safe when we reach our destination." He looked at the black house. The old woman sat in her chair again, eyes now closed, muttering to herself. Xander signalled, and the party moved on through the town. They stopped at the Wharf Inn and booked several rooms.

Back at the black house, a fly landed on the railing of the porch in front of the old woman, whose eyes remained closed. She stopped rocking and slapped her crooked hand down on the railing with surprising speed and force, trying to crush the insect. Several bones snapped in her hand as she missed the fly, which now hovered before her. She grunted and opened her white eyes.

Murk shifted back into his natural form, revealing himself to the old Seer.

"Ah, a shapeshifter," Zinduk spat. "Clever. I thought your kind were gone."

"I believe I am the last," the Dark Elf said, studying the old woman with his black eyes. A smile formed on his pale, scarred face. "I am surprised you could sense me in that tiny form. Very few can."

"The stench of your evil carries far, Dark Elf," she grunted. "Your shifty nature hides you in the prophecies. Not even I could see you." She sighed. "We all have our part, I suppose, even something as filthy as you."

He stepped forward. "It is a shame I do not have time to make our meeting more memorable, you old hag. I would have enjoyed your screams."

Zinduk looked up and cackled loudly, spittle covering the front of her black dress. "Oh, just get it over with you foul, demon spawning...." Her voice cut off as a black dagger went hilt deep up through her chin, silencing her forever.

Murk pulled the blade out and cleaned it on her dress. He left her in the rocking chair, head resting on her chest, absently wondering how long it would take the townsfolk to notice she was dead. A moment later, a fly flew off the porch towards town.

13

Xander awoke in the morning to more death. The young soldier Tom and his roommate both had their throats slashed. This time, their hearts and internal organs were missing. The wizard looked grim, surveying the scene. He turned to the others who had gathered around. "Someone is taking us out a little at a time. They are toying with us, removing the guards first. No magic was used to enter this room, or I would have sensed it. After the men retired for the night, I placed a ward on all the doors, but it wasn't triggered."

Xander noticed the window shutters had no lock, but they were on the inn's second floor. Surely, a murderer could not leap out of a window and close it at the same time. Could someone have already been in the room? If so, where had they gone? The questions remained unanswered.

They were two days away from the Guild, which left them only one more night exposed to the elements and whatever was hunting them. The old Seer, Zinduk, had felt an evil with them. She had looked at the young guard, Tom, but now he was dead. Could he have been infected with something? No, she had sensed a presence.

She was sensitive to things even he could not feel.

Xander sighed, looking at the dead men. He remembered what Zinduk had told him and his Protector sixteen summers ago when they journeyed to Vanalon from the Guild. It was one of the main reasons he moved to the small city in the first place, besides investigating the red-eyed baby. Zinduk had information only he knew, verifying that her Telling was true.

She had told him, "Heed the queen's message. The boy is the one. He must suffer first to know love. Do not intercede until you must, and must you will. Then his training can begin." The Seer had paused, studying him with white eyes. "You are a relic, old man. Arkan saved the world. You cannot do the same. Only the boy can, though the hope is faint. I will see you once more."

That made the wizard smile. He could break her prophecy right now by going back through town and seeing her a second time. It did not feel right though. They needed to make haste to reach the Guild by the following evening. He smiled inwardly, feeling like a pawn of prophecy.

"We must go," Xander said, looking at the rest of his companions, who stood with white faces, still disturbed by the new deaths. They were now down to six guards, including the captain. "Ready the horses. I will talk with the owner and pay him to give the men a proper burial. Given the circumstances, we must ride hard today and spend one more night outdoors before reaching the safety of the Guild. I do not know what stalks us, but we must be alert." Captain Melvin saluted and left to ready their mounts. Xander looked at the death scene one more time, his mind racing. Something was hunting them, and it was no mere demon.

SHORTLY AFTER, they rode out of town. The party did not eat breakfast. Nobody except Chase, who could eat at any time, had an appetite for food after seeing the defiled bodies. Besides, they had eaten a considerable seafood dinner in the common room the night before, replete with all manner of fish.

Chip had never tried most of them, including eel. His favourite was the red fleshy fish called lake trout, which tasted sweet. He enjoyed trying different things, always remembering Garth's teachings. "Say yes much more than no. Always try new things, even when you are afraid. Everything you want is on the other side of fear."

The princess tried almost everything too, except the eel. No amount of coercion could get her even to smell it. She had seen it alive in a fish tank once in Toron. Its sharp teeth and malevolent face terrified her. Chip smiled, but his levity did not last. The thought of the dead soldiers left his heart heavy and troubled. Something was hunting them that he could feel but not identify.

When the Seer Zinduk had hissed, Chip realized that an evil presence was somehow with them, but he could not see it. Then, it seemed to lift after she named it. He did not understand. In any event, they only had one more night on the plains and then safety.

The road turned sharply south, hugging Lake Supper on its way to Toron. This was their cue to leave. The party left the road and continued east to the Wizard's Guild, following a wide path created by farmers and hunters. The wheat fields were finally gone, replaced by a variety of different crops.

The horses maintained a steady trot all morning through pumpkin patches and apple orchards. The sun was out, but a dark storm gathered behind them. It rarely rained on the Great Plains, but now, near the foothills, the weather changed frequently. Due to severe storms, Garth said many ships had settled on the bottom of Lake Supper.

The wind began to intensify, turning cooler. Above them, the boy heard a raven give off a sharp shriek. Up ahead, a yellow forest with a golden hue appeared in front of them. As they got closer, Chip realized it was cornfields.

MURK FLEW high above the party, assuming the shape of a raven. It was a smaller bird but cunning and agile. From this vantage point, he could see great distances. The Dark Elf had found something disturbing the night before while gathering information from a local tavern. The Wizard's Guild had moved from the southern part of the Troll Kingdom to its current location, a day's ride north of Toron. From Thundar, it was only two days away.

When the boy wizard and his companions broke east off the road, Murk finally knew where they were headed. The soldiers guarding them all seemed to think they were going to Toron. The old wizard was crafty and hid their destination well. Murk did not like surprises. He had less time than anticipated.

The Dark Elf had been toying with them, culling the herd. He did not want to risk taking out the magic wielders yet. He preferred to isolate them more, so he focused on the guards. He also enjoyed picking them off one by one.

Now, events forced him to play his hand. Once they reached the Guild, killing and capturing would be more difficult. He admonished himself for toying with them so long. He had always loved to play the game. When they camped in the evening, he would make his move. He would transform and take out the Protectors first, then crush the others.

Up ahead, Murk suddenly saw something he could not resist using to his advantage. He liked to plan everything, but sometimes, an opportunity would arise that was too good to pass up. He would relay a message to his trackers, who were not far behind, instructing them to attack when the moment was right. They could injure the boy and wizard as much as they wished, but it was essential to leave them alive. If lucky, he could take out the princess and Protectors in one fell swoop. As the party approached the cornfields, the raven screamed with a rush of pleasure.

THE HORSES HAD to go single file between the rows of corn. The plants were close to seven feet tall, ready for harvest. The wind, strong a moment before, disappeared into an eerie calm. All sounds muted as they moved forward. Chip immediately felt claustrophobic as the view turned yellow in all directions.

The weapons master kept the horses at a steady pace, wishing to put the fields behind them. They rode for a long while in silence. Above them, dark storm clouds moved in. It was likely windy around the fields, but inside, nothing moved. The boy could not shake a sense of dread. It felt like there was evil in these fields. He looked around, feeling the plants pressing in on him.

Suddenly, a mournful howl sounded close by, causing his heart to beat wildly. It was a warning from Silvermane. Something was coming.

Garth held up his hand. The horses stopped. The weapons master put a finger to his lips. Chip tried to find the Calm. They all heard a faint snap then a rustling several rows over. Trying to tell which direction the noise came from was difficult. Another snap sounded on what seemed to be the opposite side. Garth drew his sword, and the others followed. More faint sounds and rustles could be heard, growing louder. The noise was now coming from all directions. Chip heard something breathing a couple of rows over, making his heart lurch.

A dark figure sprang across the rows, pulling the guard ahead of him clean off his horse. Another black mass flew behind him, taking out the rear soldier. The boy broke through the Wall, seizing his Power, and shielded himself and the princess.

Noise exploded everywhere. Demons suddenly surrounded them, shrieking and clawing. The horses bolted, running in different directions. Some of the black creatures were knocked aside or trampled. Chip saw Eleanor disappear into the rows. Long claws tore another guard off his horse nearby.

The boy saw a muscular demon with large jaws bite deep into the riderless horse's neck, which instantly fountained blood. Chip's terrified mount carried him headlong through row upon row of corn. He frantically tried to reign in the beast, feeling the princess slipping away. He still had her shielded, but his hold was loosening as her horse ran in the opposite direction.

Chip sensed Eleanor fill with her Power, which reassured him, and then an enormous wall of muscle knocked him and his horse completely over.

Wrapped in the shield, he withstood the impact but tumbled end over end. The boy sprang to his feet in time to see his horse dragged violently away. It disappeared from view. Chip ran forward, leaping through several corn rows and found its head but no body. His rage ignited, and he almost incinerated everything around him but realized it would kill his friends too.

As the thought entered his mind, a long black tail whipped around ferociously and struck him on the side, knocking him through several rows. He righted himself, gripping his sword with white knuckles. He had no idea where he was. Fear and a strong feeling of claustrophobia struck him as the yellow corn stalks pressed in. His view was the same everywhere he looked.

Chip's hold on the Power weakened, but he thought of the princess unprotected, and a helpless rage overtook him. The boy started running, but it was all the same. He managed to find some broken corn stalks with bright red blood on them. Then he heard screams coming from different directions and bodies thrown violently. Abruptly, a loud voice rang out in the distance. "To me, to me." It was the weapons master.

At first, he did not know which direction the voice was coming from, but the second call allowed him to pinpoint that it was some distance to his right. He heard a shuffling and a grunt, and then a figure ran headlong into him. It was Captain Melvin. Great gashes ran across his face and chest. Something huge and black was coming up behind him. Chip finally had a target.

He reached over the injured man's shoulder and sent a stream of red fire lancing into the black thing. Quick as a thought, it darted sideways and disappeared. He could not believe something could move that fast. He turned to the captain, who was shaking uncontrollably, and sent healing Power into his body, reforming his face and sealing his wounds.

A sharp scream sounded behind him. The princess! He felt magic shoot out and then heard a loud thump. He ran full speed back in the direction of the scream to find Eleanor struggling on the ground under a mass of black creatures. Long, sinewy demons were tearing at her body, barely prevented by a wavering brown shield. Crouched over them all was a monstrous thing out of a nightmare.

Two wings folded across its broad back. The giant demon looked more like a wasp than anything else. The beast pushed aside its smaller brethren and snapped long jaws with sharp fangs around Eleanor's body, lifting the girl in the air. It shook her viciously. Somehow, it could withstand the pain of her magic though its mouth smoked. Chip could feel her hold of the Power slipping as her fear took over. The fangs sunk deeper as the shield weakened, finally puncturing deep into her soft skin. She screamed.

The boy unleashed a stream of red fire at the beast's side. With unnatural speed, the creature cunningly flung her at him, but not before his magic struck them both. It hit her shield, destroying it and burning her. The princess flew into him, knocking Chip over. He released his shield to avoid burning her further.

At least his red magic stream had struck the wasp-like demon in its side. As fast as it was, it could not avoid contact with his Power. The force sent it careening off into the field. He instinctively wrapped the princess and himself in a new shield, laying her flat. He saw deep puncture marks on her neck, and blood was coming out of her chest. The girl's side was badly burned and smoking from his Power. She was having trouble breathing. More demons came at them, tearing and clawing. He did not even look at them. Chip strengthened his shield and focused only on her. She began spitting up blood and convulsing.

The boy was stricken by an overwhelming feeling of panic that he was the one who ended her life. His Power had killed her. The thought almost made him lose his grip on reality, and his magic wavered. A demon's hand got through and slashed his neck, cutting deep. He looked at her as his blood dripped down and mixed with hers. She was gasping for air. His whole world began to waver and falter. It was all his fault. The weight of the mass of demons tearing at him in the oppressive cornfields felt claustrophobic.

Another talon pierced his weakening shield, tearing a long rent in his cheek, spilling more blood. Chip felt his Power slipping away. At the same time, the wasp-like demon came back for him, jaws open. He looked at it in terror, realizing he was about to die.

As the demon insect closed its jaws over him, a large silver form hurtled from the side straight into the wasp, snapping fangs around its neck. The force sent both crashing across multiple cornrows, limbs flailing. It was the mountain wolf, giving him a chance. Sharp teeth bit into the boy's shoulder and neck as his shield failed.

The sacrifice Silvermane was making exploded his anxious thoughts apart, igniting his rage and snapping him out of his fear. He looked at the princess, convulsing in terror as her life slipped away. Blood leaked from his many wounds, and he shook from the pain. Yet, the rage of losing her swept over him. Chip strengthened his shield, burning any demon that tried to break through.

He turned the rest into healing energy that filled her body. He had watched Miss Owl do it to the weapons master. He would do the same. Behind him, he felt demons slashing at his body from all sides and then heard screams of pain as their claws melted. He vaguely heard Xander in the background, yelling.

"Protect them!" Blue fire lanced out in several directions. The weapons master leapt over him, swinging like crazy. Chase was there too, covered in blood, fighting with his bare hands. Chip forced himself to focus.

The princess looked at him with fear in her eyes, blood coming out of her mouth as she tried to breathe. He dissolved the blood in her lungs, pumping fresh air in. Even as he did, more blood filled them up, and she struggled again. He repeated the process, but it was not working. He needed to find the source of the injury. He moved away from her lungs, allowing blood to flow back in, hearing her choke. He knew he only had moments.

He moved his mind around her chest, trying to find the source. He could not find it. She started seizing, and then he sensed a small hole in a major vein. He sealed it and removed the blood again, allowing her to gasp for breath.

Despite his efforts, he realized her blood loss was too pronounced. She was getting weaker, her grip loosening as she lost consciousness. Her eyes closed.

The orphan, with eyes blazing, clenched his hands in utter frustration as he watched the princess die. He saw his own blood dripping from his face and neck and then, out of desperation, used it to fill her body. A weakness washed over him, but he ignored it. Chip used his blood to make her organs function properly and then focused on her other wounds. Eleanor's eyes remained closed as he repaired the puncture marks in her neck and chest, reforming her veins. Finally, he sloughed off her burnt skin and replaced it. He sat back, spent.

She opened her eyes. A flood of emotions overtook him, led by joy. He hugged her and then turned his attention around him, seeing dead demons everywhere. Chase was lying on the ground, not moving. Xander bent over him, sending blue magic into his body. Garth stood to the side, sword raised, with a gash in his chest and leg, awaiting any more attackers. Captain Melvin was still alive, sitting between two rows, clutching his stomach.

The cornfields had gone silent. Above them, dark clouds blocked the sun.

Chip rose and rushed to his best friend but stumbled as a spell of dizziness engulfed him. He realized he had lost much blood but did not care. He shrugged off the pain and nausea and knelt next to Xander. He gasped, looking at his childhood friend. The tall boy's wounds were grave.

"He is on the cusp," Xander said, looking doubtful. "Link with me." Chip immediately gave access to his Power. The wizard used it to shore up large rents in the boy's chest and stomach. His heart was fluttering from loss of blood. The old man turned, exhausted. "I fear he is too far gone. He needs blood. Do you have the strength?" Chip nodded, not bothering to think about it. This was his best friend. Xander pulled more blood out of Chip, using it to restart the tall boy's organs, then sealed a ruptured lung and regulated his heartbeat. The wizard slumped back and waited.

Chase gasped, then took deep, regular breaths. Xander let out a loud sigh of relief. He then looked with concern at the orphan, who started smiling despite the rent in his cheek. Chip realized he could not feel the pain anymore. Somehow, he could not maintain the hold on his Power either. He tried to move, but nothing worked. A wave of blackness enveloped him as he fell backwards. His last thought was that at least the princess and his best friend were safe.

MURK STRUGGLED with the mountain wolf, rolling end over end. Its jaws were fastened tightly around the neck of his demon form. He desperately wanted to use his magic, but it would alert the others that he was a shapeshifter. He reminded himself that he had taken the form of one of the deadliest demons ever created.

The insect-like wasp had almost metallic armour, which was extremely difficult to pierce and much stronger against magic. It was the reason the wolf had not killed him yet. The animal's fangs could not penetrate his skin, though eventually it would. He needed to defeat the beast in this form, which should have been easy, but he struggled.

The wolf was savage and massive, unlike any he had ever seen. His side also burned terribly from the boy's red Power. He pulled his clawed three-toed feet up and wind-milled them into the wolf's stomach, causing great rents in its flesh. The animal grunted then shook his neck harder, swinging him around and slamming him on the ground. Murk's vision blurred, pain ratcheting through his demon form. The animal noticed the burn hole in his side and used its great paws to dig in and tear it open further. The Dark Elf gritted his teeth in agony as black blood leaked out. In desperation, he clasped his foreclaws around the giant dog's neck and squeezed with all his might. He felt his long nails break through the beast's skin, sinking deep into its massive neck. Red blood covered his claws, and the dog finally released its death grip.

The mountain wolf turned, pulling away, then bit savagely into his side. Murk clenched his teeth, seeing stars, and scuttled backwards. The beast would not let go. He turned and was finally able to bring his great jaws around and fasten them around the wolf's bloody neck. Murk tasted warm blood and heard it whimper. With a massive effort, the huge beast used its paws to push away from him, gouging him further. He felt more flesh tear on the dog's neck as it escaped his jaws. The wolf stood up, leaking blood everywhere. The shapeshifter squirmed on his back in pain, sucking in ragged breaths of air, waiting.

Murk had fought many battles in his life. He could sense when the tide had turned, and victory was in his grasp. He could not believe how savage and powerful this animal was. Twice, it had alerted the boy and his companions to his attacks. The Dark Elf wondered why. He wanted to use his magic to look at its memories but could not risk it. As he looked into its great eyes, he watched it stumble. Blood leaked out of its neck and stomach.

Murk knew the end was near. He also knew what it was about to do. With a low growl, the monstrous wolf leapt high into the air with jaws open. It was precisely what the Dark Elf was waiting for.

As it tried to land on him, he brought his armoured wasp tail straight up with frightening speed, impaling the mountain wolf through the heart as it came down. The beast slid along his tail, coming to rest in the air just above him. He looked into its eyes and watched the life leave them.

A thrill coursed through his body. He whipped his muscled tail sideways, throwing the dog's dead body to the side. Murk looked at his wound, still leaking blood. He wanted to go back and finish the others, but he was too injured. The girl was likely dead and one of the Protectors, but otherwise, the mountain wolf had spoiled his plans. Murk had miscalculated.

He forced himself to his feet and staggered away, gritting his teeth while he held his side. He knew by the silence that all his trackers and muscled demons were dead. The Dark Elf would have to heal and regroup. He would be patient. It was a necessary virtue for an assassin.

Murk would not fail again.

END OF VOLUME 4.

IF YOU ENJOYED READING THIS, please leave a review on Amazon. It would be greatly appreciated.

Visit my website: www.terryironwood.com

Type your email address at the bottom of the page to be notified of my next book launch.

I have added a free short story prequel called "Weapons Master" in the upper right corner of my website. It is Garth Stone's backstory.

The Orphan's Quest audiobook with special effects is now available on Audible.

Link to Volume Five: Wizard's Guild

I hope you enjoyed Volume 4: Guardian. Be sure to look out for Volumes 5 to 7 of The Great Forget Fantasy Series!

The Great Forget Fantasy Series:

Volume 1: Orphan's Quest

Volume 2: Defenders of Hope

Volume 3: A Dim World

Volume 4: Guardian

Volume 5: Wizard's Guild

Volume 6: Stone Kingdom

Volume 7: Coming end of December, 2024.

Acknowledgements

I offer my heartfelt thanks to my family and friends, who provided invaluable support, wisdom, and encouragement. You know who you are. I especially want to mention Kevin C., Steve S., and Ward C., who went above and beyond.

I am delighted to work with my editor, Jason Letts from Imbue Editing, who continues to improve my writing.

Last, and certainly not least, I wish to thank an orphan, Chip, for taking me on his quest.

Many thanks,
Terry Ironwood

ABOUT THE AUTHOR

Terry Ironwood resides with his family. He holds multiple university degrees and is interested in the science of self-improvement. He is equally fascinated with physics and spirituality. Terry believes in an 'attitude of gratitude' and is grateful he can write full-time. His dream is to help others reach their full potential.

Printed in Dunstable, United Kingdom